EMP EXODUS
Dark New World: Book 2

JJ HOLDEN
&
HENRY GENE FOSTER

Copyright © 2016 by JJ Holden / Henry Gene Foster
All rights reserved.
www.jjholdenbooks.com

This is a work of fiction. All of the characters, organizations, and events portrayed in this novel are either products of the author's imagination or are used fictitiously.

ISBN: 1533003998
ISBN-13: 978-1533003997

EMP EXODUS

- 1 -

2200 HOURS - ZERO DAY +5

ETHAN SHOWED THE others the third section of his bunker, which he thought of as the dorm. It had sixteen individual bunks stacked two-high along the walls, and not much else. There were also the supply section and the living section.

Unfortunately, they'd have to leave almost immediately if they wanted to avoid follow-up patrols by the invaders. Sooner or later the enemy would find the bunker, and it would be over for them all if they weren't long gone by then.

Still, he was glad he'd been able to broadcast vital intelligence to the Resistance groups, courtesy of "the 20s." He thanked the heavens that he'd thought to bring relays and wire, and all the components needed to make that broadcast appear to have come from somewhere other than his bunker. He tried not to think about the civilians who must have died in the terrible bombing the enemy gave Chesterbrook when they took out his broadcast equipment—which he'd been smart enough to place far away from his actual bunker. Those people would likely have starved soon anyway, he told himself, and at least bombing was a quick death compared to that poisonous brown gunk they sprayed.

Putting the broadcast equipment far from the bunker hadn't helped avoid the risk of detection, however, since enemy soldiers had followed Frank and his "clan" to Ethan's own house outside of town. Ethan had saved the clan, but in doing so, he guaranteed eventual discovery by the enemy.

"I'm telling you, we have to leave, and we need to do it right away," Ethan said gravely. "If we don't, we'll all die. Those soldiers *will come back*."

Cassy, the newcomer who seemed to detest pretty young Jasmine, and who seemed to have just sort of taken over the clan in the single day since she'd arrived, nodded emphatically. "Yes, we do have to leave. We should take what we can and go to my homestead. As I said, it's just north of Lancaster. We can walk there. I have a bunker at the ranch, too, and about twenty man-years of long-term food storage. Not to mention a seed vault with my stockpile of so many seeds and local growth saplings it'll make your head spin."

Frank asked, "Do you think your five acres can feed all twelve of us, Cassy?" It wasn't a challenge, Ethan noted, but a simple, practical question.

Cassy grinned. "I do what's called intensive gardening—sustainable agriculture on a pretty big scale. I can raise about six thousand pounds of food on less than a quarter-acre," she declared with obvious pride. "But it doesn't look at all like the farms you're used to. It looks more like a weed-filled jungle."

Frank nodded. "Good enough for me, Cassy. Good enough for my family. When do we leave?"

Ethan cleared his throat. "We should leave in the morning, no later. We'll need time first to inventory what I have and split up what we have to bring. Unfortunately, I have to bring my computer to Cassy's farm, to continue my work. I can't talk about the details, but I'm helping the

Resistance organize and coordinate. Without people like me, they wouldn't stand a chance."

Cassy said, "I have a top-end laptop in a faraday cage in my bunker, Ethan. You can use that, so long as it won't bring danger to my farm. Radios, too—a dozen short-range and a good HAM radio."

Ethan paused to consider this, then said, "Perfect, actually. Then I only need to bring a thumb drive with my files and programs. We'll bring a few of my own hand-held radios, too, for the trip. Do you have wire or signal relays?"

"I have lots of wire in different gauges, but I don't know what a signal relay is."

Ethan shrugged. "Okay, then I'll need to bring half a dozen Raspberry Pi modules. They're small enough to fit in an Altoids tin, so they're light and easy. Carrying a spool of wire and a HAM radio would have been a bitch."

For the rest of the day, Ethan led the clan in gathering food and supplies for the journey. He also checked and rechecked that he had everything he'd need to set up his satellite linkup and broadcasting once they got there. It was a lot of stuff to pack, and they didn't get to sleep until late in the night.

* * *

0900 HOURS - ZERO DAY +6

With increasing impatience, Peter Ixin sat encamped within a copse of trees and waited for his prey to emerge. The woman had led the invaders right to his community of farmers, yet he'd almost caught her before she got away. Just when he was about to take her down, a rookie scout on his team had gotten herself killed, and the spy woman took the scout's rifle, which then led to Peter's concussion and allowed the bitch to escape altogether.

Peter had managed to get out of medical imprisonment and then caught up with the scouts who had been sent after the spy, sure, but then the Enemy had come. The invaders bombed his community and sprayed the fields with something brown and noxious. In all the noise, the spy had escaped a second time.

He had almost caught up to her yet again when she was badly wounded by an exploding vehicle, and some new person had emerged from the smoke to complicate the picture and saved her. Spy and savior had disappeared into the smoke together, and Peter hadn't yet found the entry hatch they must surely have gone through. No way she could have escaped through the smoke on her own, in her condition—she had to be underground, maybe in a bunker, and now she wasn't alone. She had help.

Peter, however, was alone, having sent the scout team he'd commandeered home. At this point, they would only get in the way and alert his prey. Maybe they would find enough of their community intact to salvage some pieces, but he doubted it.

Well, maybe he couldn't get justice for the invaders, but he could damn sure get justice on that woman for killing someone under his command and for leading the invaders straight to them. Bitch. But if she didn't come out of her hidey-hole soon he'd have to leave to find more food and water, and then she might escape...again.

His stomach growled, protesting his careful supply rationing, and Peter considered just how long he could remain in place. Then in the morning light, he saw movement. A man moved like a ghost through the remaining smoke and fog. It must be the man who had saved the spy. Peter watched as the man seemed to glide across the field from cover to cover, stopped for one minute here, another minute there, then moved on. Soon the man returned to the middle of the field, stooped down, and disappeared.

A thrill went up Peter's spine, and he lost all thoughts of leaving just yet. He was a patient man—one of his best character traits, in his opinion—and he sat rock-still as he looked through his binoculars at the field. Hell, he'd already been there for God knew how many hours. A few more wouldn't kill him. His heart began to race when his hunter's patience was rewarded, as it so often had been throughout his life. First one person, then another and another filtered out from whatever hole they had hidden in, moving in a single-file line away toward the south.

His eyes went wide when he saw what they carried. Every one of the adults had an M4 and two backpacks, one in front and another on their backs, both of them stuffed to the brim. Radios and bottles and pouches dangled from ties so they appeared loaded down like mules. His spirits leapt. If they carried this much stuff with them, they must have left twice that much behind. Even better, they moved like they had somewhere to go. Somewhere safer and better supplied, Peter decided. *And the woman spy was among them*; icing on the cake.

A thought hit him, and he frowned. Should he go back to the Farms and let them know about the cache, and gather more scouts to track the spy and her companions? Or should he trail them first to see where they went, and then return to the Farms for help?

Peter clenched his jaw and made his decision. He'd follow that woman wherever she went on God's Earth and then go back for his own people. They could leave their bombed and blighted fields. Peter would lead them to whatever land of plenty the spy was headed toward, and he'd be the savior of his people, Moses leading his people out of the wilderness... and *then* that bitch would die.

- 2 -

1000 HOURS - ZERO DAY +6

TAGGART SAT WITH Pvt. Eagan, one of the three members of his unit who had survived thus far. They ate a can of chili and a can of peaches each, courtesy of the Resistance, as they awaited a meeting with one of the Resistance leaders.

Eagan said, "Look, Sarge, I mean Captain. I'll follow your orders ahead of anyone else's no matter what their rank is. I was just wondering if that major had the authority to give you a field promotion."

Taggart was silent a moment as he thought about how to respond and finally said, "Eagan, I got no doubts about your loyalty. You never did give a shit about chain of command, you unsat shitbird, so I trust you. But yeah, I think he did have the authority. I mean, we ran around with him all day yesterday, and then through the night picking up stragglers and survivors from other units. I have no idea how these Resistance guys got the intel about their locations—one of them said something about a group called the 20s."

He glanced over at Eagan. "However they get their intel, it was mostly accurate. How many soldiers have we saved, twenty or so? We have most of a platoon now, scattered through half a dozen Resistance safe houses. I'm the one holding the intel, the one who did the saving, and now the highest ranking soldier among us. It would have been the major, but he ate a grenade to get that last group away to safety with you and me. I think we better honor that field promotion he gave me. He won't be handing out any more of them."

Eagan stuffed his mouth with chili and didn't continue until he'd swallowed it. "So what you're saying, Cap, is that this major saw enough of what's going on to think you were the most battlefield-expedient option for leading a crew of soon-to-be-dead soldiers? What with him dying next and all."

"Pretty much. Who is it says, 'Adapt, Improvise, and Overcome'? That's the long and short of it."

"That'd be the jarheads, sir," Eagan replied with a grin, though he skipped a beat before adding the courtesy "sir."

Calling Taggart "Captain" and "Sir" would take getting used to for Eagan and his other three guys, but Taggart also knew that the FNGs—fucking new guys—would never know the difference. Especially not with him wearing the Captain's Bars the major had handed him just before the poor guy went out in a blaze of glory. Now, by God, he had over thirty grunts under him, in different safe houses, each with local Resistance liaisons. Every team had radios, which Taggart learned the 20s had stashed in galvanized garbage cans. Somehow—he didn't understand the explanation really—this had kept the radios safe and functional through the EMP wave. Inexpensive civilian models but they worked just fine.

Taggart's thoughts and his meal were interrupted by a knock on the door to the bedroom where he and Pvt. Eagan were encamped. He looked up, calling, "Enter."

The door swung open, and his liaison came in, smiling. "Sir, please let me introduce the man you've been waiting to meet, Mr. Black—not his real name, of course. He's a subleader in the Resistance. It's his patronage that got you these quarters, intelligence, food and ammo, so in effect, you're under his command. 'Temporary Additional Duty,' he calls it. Anyway, Mr. Black, this is now-Captain Taggart, the guy commanding those grunts we got holing up in your houses."

Mr. Black, ironically, was just a touch lighter than midnight in complexion. He wore baggy jeans with some sort of silly civilian imprint, expensive white sneakers with blue accents, and a black net wife-beater shirt. He topped it all off with a damn ridiculous fedora. To Taggart, it seemed a rather silly costume, but Black radiated an iron confidence that suggested he'd had a hard and violent life. That might be good, given their new realities. Taggart decided it would be best to show him at least a pretense of respect, if only for his importance to the mission.

"Mr. Black. Although my boys and girls are outside of any kind of official chain of command, I welcome you, and I am glad to finally meet you."

Mr. Black frowned. "Shut the fuck up, soulja boy. I don't give two shits about you or your posse, other than they can help my cause. You got me?"

Taggart laughed out loud, then struggled to regain his composure. "Mister, I understand you completely. You're a fucking civilian wearing a wannabe gangsta cover—that means hat—and you look like a fucking cartoon. But you're in charge here, and you earned it somehow, so, either way, we're in your debt. Bark away little Chihuahua. I'll listen to you, and my grunts will listen to me. So now I'll ask *you* if we're clear."

Mr. Black first grinned and then let out a belly laugh. "Oh yeah, grunt. I get you. We'll get along fine. Don't much like you, but I need you, and you sure as fuck need me. Yeah, we'll get along like applesauce."

Whatever that meant. "So what's the SITREP, Mr. Black? What can we do for each other?"

"Two things. First, you already know that the 411 we gave you about where to find more soldiers came from the 20s. We got no idea who they are, but they been right by us with everything they give us so far. Keep an eye out for anything that might help figure who they are."

Well, that much was obvious, and Taggart already wanted to know who they were. So, it would be easy to agree to that. He nodded. "Roger that. Anything else?"

Mr. Black continued, "And thing two is, we need you to run licks for us when we got targets."

"What the fuck is a lick?" asked Taggart. Pvt. Eagan coughed, probably trying to keep himself from laughing, and Black rolled his eyes.

"We got lots of info from the 20s," Black told Taggart. "Invader troop movements, supply caches, that sorta thing. I want you runnin' and gunnin' to get those supplies, and run some ambushes. Run a lick, grab what you can, and fade. Crystal?"

"Yes. We can do that. The fact is, mister, I want to use my groups to harass the enemy so much their soldiers have to guard caches and look for us, not be out there conquering America and squeezing civilians."

Mr. Black grinned, the smile getting wider and wider as Taggart spoke. "Soulja boy, let me tell you about the first supplies you gonna grab out."

As Black went into details, Taggart's face gradually took on a nasty, predatory grin.

* * *

1300 HOURS - ZERO DAY +6

Frank sat with the rest of his newly expanded clan as they ate lunch. Michael wasn't present since he had gone out a half hour before to scout after Cassy said there were roads and settlements ahead, going by her local map.

Sipping at his water, Frank heard the warbling call of a quail. That would be Michael returning, notifying the clan he was coming in so no one got jumpy and shot at him. Frank stood, wiping dirt from his jeans, and waited for Michael to arrive.

"Welcome back," he said when he saw the former Marine scout. "Find out anything useful?"

Michael spat. "Sure did. Reese Road, going north to south, with houses and little businesses on it as far north as I went. There's people there, too, all of 'em armed. They were hiding, but not well enough."

Frank frowned. "Damn. Well, we knew we'd find people eventually. This little forest we've been walking through couldn't last forever. Can we go around to the south?"

"Negative. I-76 is over that way, and the Pennsylvania Turnpike. People with guns are on the turnpike, too. It's a mess."

Cassy shifted the sling that held up her wounded arm and stepped toward them. So no one else could hear her, she said in a near-whisper, "We can't go south of I-76, either. There are more towns along the south side of 76, and there's a group of whack-job armed farmers somewhere down there, too. I don't exactly know where. Could be I ran across their main encampment when they shot at me, but we can't take the chance that I only stumbled into a temporary camp. They were bad dudes, shooting first and asking questions never. I was lucky I got away, and I'm pretty damn sure they were still tracking me when the van blew up next to me, and

Michael saved my life."

Michael nodded, acknowledging her and her information. "Well then, we have to dogleg north a bit and try to thread the needle—there is a thin strip of trees running between an auto body shop and the next house down. With luck, the trees won't be guarded. Everyone, check your weapons and make sure you're on single-fire. I'll double check each rifle to make sure we're squared away. Fire discipline isn't something I can teach in five minutes, but this will make sure you don't burn through ammo. And don't shoot unless I yell for covering fire, or fighting already started, and you have a real clear shot."

He paused for a sip of the water Frank offered him, then continued: "We will move out at dusk. There's enough light for us to see where we are going, but will make it harder for them to notice us."

Frank clenched his jaw. The odds of a small, in-town strip of woods being unguarded, when Michael had already seen people in the buildings to either side, were pretty small, dammit. He had to make sure everyone was on high alert when they went through. Maybe he should tell his clan to shoot anything that moved? No, that wasn't what the clan was about. But they'd sure as hell better draw down on anything that moved and looked armed. And of course, Michael would have to be up front, catching any surprise heat.

Sometime soon he'd have to set Michael up to mentor at least one other person in the skills and tactics that he'd picked up in the Middle East, but for now, Michael had to make announcements about how to proceed. And goddamn if he knew why the scout had suddenly stepped into a leadership role with these misfits—his friends and family, as far as you could get from military discipline. As long as they were in a nearly combat environment that was fine, but

Frank knew that as soon as they were safe, Michael would step back again, and leadership would fall on him once again. Cassy better heal quick, he decided, so he could drop this dog turd of a job onto her and hope she saw it as peaches and ice cream.

* * *

Cassy accepted Frank's plan without comment. She doubted she could come up with a better one. It grated that he put her in charge of herding the children, but with her arm in a sling, she could only fire her pistol. The M4 over her left shoulder, which Ethan had passed to her from his stockpile, was just a decoration until she healed up enough to use it.

Hell, she was just happy to be able to keep up with the group, given the severity of her wounds. The metal shard that impaled her right shoulder at the joint had done some serious soft tissue damage, and no one could say how fully it would heal. For now, it was stable, and she had plenty of Percocet and antibiotics from Ethan's medical supplies. Yippee!

She saw her mother edge toward her as they finished preparing to move out. "Hey Mom," Cassy said. "What's up?"

Grandma Mandy, as the kids called her, smiled. "How are you holding up, honey? The kids and I worry, you know."

"C'mon, Mom. I'm fine. It hurts, but I made it this far. I won't crap out on you guys. But you knew that already. What do you really want?"

"Fine, sweetie. The kids and I want to know if you'll join us in a prayer before we get walking again. From what I overheard, the next little bit of our journey could be rough, and they need reassurance. The Lord will provide if they only ask Him."

Cassy fought an urge to roll her eyes and managed to

keep her reaction in check. Praying to God would not help them, she figured, but it might help her kids. And anyway, it couldn't hurt to throw a word upstairs to the Big Guy. "Okay, Mom. We can use all the help we can get, right? I'm in."

Mandy smiled and led her to the kids. They all grabbed hands and stood in a circle as Mandy led the prayer. Cassy couldn't help but notice how her mom seemed somehow stronger, more potent, while she prayed. That was probably just a trick of her imagination.

Just as importantly, Cassy noted that her thirteen-year-old daughter, Brianna, and her seven-year-old son, Aidan, seemed to stand straighter, more confidently, as they prayed with Mandy. Cassy herself was conflicted about the idea of God, but Grandma Mandy had zero doubts. That stark confidence seemed almost to permeate the kids, now; where before they had been beaten, terrified, constantly worried about losing their mom or their grandma, they transformed into confident, hopeful people, and Cassy grinned at the sight.

Lost in her thoughts, she almost missed the end of the prayer and hastily replied, "Amen" with her kids. And it was time to move out.

- 3 -

1400 HOURS - ZERO DAY +6

CAPT. TAGGART MOVED from cover to cover with Eagan behind him. Two soldiers they'd picked up earlier followed behind Eagan. They'd all ditched their uniforms and were now dressed like normal civilians, only carrying pistols and a few grenades. Being out of uniform without rifles made Taggart uneasy, but dammit, uniforms were not the right garb for running and gunning "licks," guerrilla-style.

Taggart stopped at the corner of an older brick building. He recognized a row of gouges in the brickwork as bullet holes. Four evenly-spaced, dry blood stains showed that it was probably an execution. The enemy was shooting anyone too old or too young to work, or who had disabilities. Fuck, the bastards were mowing down able-bodied adults, too, when they rounded up more than they needed. The word was that they were breaching random buildings and just taking however many people they needed for one task or another. Then they simply killed whoever was left. Slave labor beat dying, Taggart figured, but not by much.

The sound of an engine reached him. When he motioned his three soldiers to take cover, they hid behind a dumpster.

Ten seconds later, a Jeep-like vehicle Taggart didn't recognize rolled by with four enemy soldiers within, their rifles pointed in all directions, faces masked with black shemaghs. Taggart fought the urge to open fire on it. The vehicle was not part of their orders, and opening fire recklessly would only draw more of the enemy to this area—the last thing he wanted right now. This mission wasn't a sweep-and-clear. They were going to retrieve a cache of ammunition and medical supplies hidden in an apartment building that was one of the points of interest they'd learned of from their mysterious 20s contact. The word was, they'd hidden it before the lights went out, and that made Taggart briefly wonder what they'd known ahead of time—and who they really were.

Once the enemy vehicle had passed and turned a corner, Taggart breathed easier and motioned his soldiers to move out. All over the city of New York, similar scenes were playing out with his other thirty or so soldiers, who now led about as many civilian Resistance fighters as well as troops. Taggart had the only unit with no civilians, but his was also the day's most important mission. The other missions were really hit-and-run raids meant to draw down enemy strength and improve the odds that Taggart's group would succeed.

Twenty minutes later they arrived at the building, a four-story brick apartment building. The once-secure entry door hung open on a single hinge, and the thick metal door bulged inward at the center. Someone had battered it down. Taggart peered into the building using a mirror to avoid exposing himself to anyone inside. The small mirror would hopefully not alert any occupants.

He need not to have worried since nothing moved inside except the flies buzzing around two bloated bodies by the mailboxes in the foyer. He didn't have time to worry about the bodies or about the stench of rot and sewage that permeated the building.

"The mission objective is in unit #309, third floor, east hallway," Taggart said. "Unknown if it's occupied. Advance by pairs. Noise discipline, soldiers. That includes you, Eagan, you little shit."

Eagan grinned, and the other two soldiers moved out. They had their pistols drawn and went up the stairs with a steady four feet of separation. The lead soldier kept his pistol aimed up the next flight of stairs, almost walking backwards to do so. As they moved up toward the second landing, Taggart and Eagan moved into position behind them on the landing they had just vacated. And so it went, flight by flight, until they reached the third floor. The lead soldier motioned that both halls were clear, then one of the pairs covered the west hallway and the other, the stairs as Taggart and Eagan flanked the east hallway.

Taggart took three deep breaths despite the stench, then he and Eagan moved down the east hallway with their backs to either wall. Fortunately, all doors in the hallway were closed. And with no need to "slice the pie" and edge across the field of view of anyone inside, hoping to see them before they saw Taggart and Eagan, progress here was faster and less dangerous than in the stairwell. If anyone popped out, he would hear the door open and have a half-second to react, knowing exactly where they were before they could know where he was.

Unit 309 was the last apartment down the long hallway. Taggart and Eagan flanked it, and Taggart steeled himself for entry.

Goddamn, entry was his absolute least favorite thing in the world. Worse than the chlamydia he got in Germany that one time. He and Eagan had practiced entries for a few minutes before leaving on this mission, which showed Taggart that Eagan knew what he was doing so he wasn't worried about his partner screwing up. But room entry got soldiers killed if the enemy was on the other side unless everything went just right.

"Showtime, Eagan," Taggart whispered with a grin, pretending an eagerness he sure didn't feel. The next three seconds would mean life or death if anyone was inside. Those three seconds always felt like an eternity to Taggart, when the adrenaline was pumping, and bullets flew.

Eagan moved away from the wall, stood in front of the door, finger-counted to three and then, without hesitation, kicked with all his might at a spot just to the inside of the door handle. The door flew open amid a shower of splinters from the door frame. Taggart ducked inside and to the right, the open door at his back; Eagan was right on his heels and rushed in to cover the other direction.

Taggart saw two soldiers sitting at the table in the apartment's breakfast nook. Their rifles leaned against the wall nearby, and their faces showed dumbfounded shock at the abrupt interruption. They died with those expressions on their faces when Taggart fired two rapid shots, double-tapping one, and then repeating that for the other. It all happened before the thought of firing crossed his mind. Years of experience had burned the reaction into his muscle memory. Four rounds down, he ticked off in his mind without a thought for the men he had just killed. Guilt never came out until dreams came at night, but these two would barely be a drop in that bucket.

Behind him, Taggart heard three shots from two weapons and spun around. Eagan had double-tapped a third soldier, who in turn had fired his rifle at the ceiling when his muscles jerked in shock and surprise. All three soldiers inside were now down.

Without another word, Taggart and Eagan swept the rest of the apartment room by room, closet by closet. They found no more soldiers, but they did find a man dead in the bathtub. They also found an unconscious woman bound and gagged in one corner, her cute yoga pants and "Talk Shit, Get Hit" halter top shredded and hanging loosely down.

Taggart clenched his jaw hard enough to hurt his teeth, eyes narrowed. "Eagan, cut this woman's bonds, and leave your MRE next to her."

Eagan nodded and did so. "Think she'll live?" he asked with a voice that sounded carefully flat and emotionless.

After a couple seconds of silence that spoke volumes, Taggart finally said, "Crowbar. The wall between the bathroom and the living room. Sense of urgency, Private."

Eagan made short work of the wall, and two PVC tubes fell out, each about two feet long and capped on both ends. "What's in them, Captain?"

"Mr. Black—what a joke he is—didn't say. He just said it was vital. Well, we have the cache."

Eagan paused and then said, "Sir, I request permission to bring the civilian with us."

Taggart frowned. "Negative, soldier. That could compromise our mission, and is outside our operational parameters. Now secure the package," he barked back. Eyes closed, the woman made no sound. Taggart gathered the dead soldiers' rifles. Any responding enemy soldiers would mow down anyone they saw in the area anyway, so secrecy was irrelevant, and the Resistance could use the arms.

"Let's get the fuck out of here, Eagan, before those bastards can send more soldiers at us." And before he had to smell one more motherfucking second of that death-filled apartment building.

* * *

2030 HOURS - ZERO DAY +6

Cassy moved as quickly as her wounded and bound shoulder would allow. Thank God the kids were smaller and also moved slower, so they set the pace for the whole "clan." Frank was a smart cookie for coming up with the clan idea since it gave the group some sort of "official" unity, a group identity that Cassy figured would probably be vital in the coming days and months.

She glanced around at the others. At the head of the group, Michael moved like a ghost, passing quickly through the trees and underbrush. He would stop and do his recon thing as the group caught up before moving ahead again. Michael was an honest-to-god Rambo as far as she was concerned. He moved the group in odd directions, but Cassy soon realized their path always took advantage of cover, or avoided walking along the crest of a hill, or skirted various hazards. Cassy prided herself on the preparedness skills she'd spent years developing, but Michael showed her on a daily basis just how limited her skills actually were when it came to defending the group.

Yes indeed, she really wished now that she'd taken more combat-focused classes. She only had some basic personal training from other preppers she knew. Well, Michael might be able to shore up her weak spots—she'd have to watch him closely, learn from him, maybe even ask him to mentor her. And he would never say no to that because he had to see that having two trained warriors and scouts was better than having just one.

To her left, Jaz and Jed walked together closely enough that she couldn't hear their quiet conversation. Michael's wife Tiffany trailed behind them a bit, her focus on the trees around them, looking for any dangers they might conceal.

To her right, Ethan and Amber were a mirror image of

Jaz and Jed, walking together. Unlike Jaz, Amber stayed alert as she walked, but Cassy could see that she and Ethan had their own quiet conversation going. Behind them, Mary and Tiffany walked in parallel a bit behind the cluster of children and Cassy.

Cassy wasn't sure what she thought of having Tiffany and Mary bring up the rear, so to speak, but the Jaz/Jed, Amber/Ethan situation sure as hell could turn into a total clusterfuck. Jaz was gorgeous, and Jed seemed to always find reasons to be near her, smiling and laughing. Amber, in turn, seemed to hover around Ethan, ostensibly to question him on a variety of survival and preparedness topics, but no one could miss how close they stood when they talked, or how often Amber laughed at Ethan's nerdy little jokes.

Worse, when Amber wasn't off to the side chatting with Ethan, she was watching Jaz and Jed like a hawk. Any time Jaz said anything, Amber would roll her eyes, or cluck, or suck her teeth. There was tension there. Yep, a total clusterfuck was coming if that "love square" got more serious. Regardless of Amber's growing friendship with Ethan, a sizzling animosity threatened any peace between Amber and Jaz. Well, mostly that was Amber since Jaz seemed oblivious. The poor girl was just used to men paying attention to her and women not liking her. It must be just so much background noise to the beautiful young woman by now.

Cassy realized she was gritting her teeth and turned her attention back to the task of guarding and guiding the young ones. This was no time to start pointing out elephants in the room. But later, after they all got to her farm? That would be a different matter. How to discreetly deal with the problem? Maybe she should talk to Frank about it. He was their reluctant leader, and plenty smart. He had a weird way of bringing everyone together and hashing out problems without starting wars.

When they got to the farm, Cassy felt certain, Frank would not resent Cassy for taking charge of the farm stuff. His leadership would be essential to getting everyone moving together on the many tasks they would face at the homestead if they wanted to get production up in the coming spring. More mouths meant more planting, more tending, more everything.

Then Cassy nearly ran into her son, Aidan, when he stopped abruptly. A quick scan of the others showed they had all stopped. Michael, up ahead, had his fist in the air. It was the signal for "stop whatever you're doing, be quiet and stay still," Michael had explained, along with a couple other hand signals. Cassy had almost missed it by wandering in her thoughts.

She watched now as Michael crouched low behind some scrub brush. She was certain it couldn't hide a person, yet somehow their scout managed to get smaller than she thought possible. He sat stone-still for several minutes and the kids got fidgety, but they stayed quiet. The adults had their rifles at the low-ready, alternating between scanning their surroundings and looking to Michael for instructions. Then Michael slinked backwards away from his concealment, moving toward the group.

Once there, he briefly and quietly spoke to Frank, then used one of the other hand signals he'd taught them, the one for "gather around" or Rally, as Michael called it. The clan quietly gathered around Michael, and he nodded at each in turn, apparently approving.

"Okay, clan, here's what's up," Michael said almost in a whisper. "Ahead is about two hundred yards of open ground, running between an occupied auto body shop on the left and a large house on the right that I think is also occupied. Our task is to get across that open terrain quickly and silently.

We'll stay low, crouching as we go. Cassy, you're injured. Can you run bent over without killing yourself or crying out in pain?"

Cassy noted how Michael asked this without apparent emotion. He was all business at the moment. If she said she couldn't do it then he'd think of another way around, she was sure, but it would be something even more dangerous than traversing open terrain between two groups of people with unknown intent. The thought scared her.

"I'll make it," Cassy said, her face expressionless. This was going to hurt like a bitch, but there was no help for it.

Ten minutes later, Michael had explained the plan, and the route he thought was best and drilled into them several times that if someone started shooting at them, they had to reach that cover before any other consideration. Getting caught in the open in a crossfire could mean death. He looked hard at them and didn't pull any punches as he spoke. No one had any doubts about their situation.

"Now," Michael continued, "listen up. Each child needs to go with an adult. If a kid gets shot, carry them. If an adult gets shot, *keep fuckin' running*. Better one down than all. I'll go after anyone down later if they're alive. If you get shot, lie still and wait until the firing stops, then look ahead for me. I won't willingly leave one of our clan behind, I promise you all. While you cross, I'll stay in position on overwatch and then follow and regroup with you once you're in the trees across the field. If the enemy fires on us, I'll be right here to take them out. Jed, you'll have to take two of the kids with you. Too dangerous for me to take one. Are we clear, and are we ready to move out?"

Silent nods all around, and the others picked the child they would move out with. Five kids. Six adults, including Cassy's daughter, Brianna. Though only thirteen, she'd have to be an adult for now because Cassy wasn't well enough to carry even Michael's five-year-old son, Nick. The task of leading Nick would fall to Jed, who would have two kids with him.

"Alright then. You all know the plan. It's time to move out. You can do this, folks. This is our clan. These are our kids and our people. *We will make it.* Don't be scared—save your fear for later. For now, it's time to man up, take a deep breath and do this."

Cassy nodded and offered up a silent prayer to a god she wasn't sure she believed in. *Please, God, let us get through this and if anything goes wrong, let the kids be safe.*

- 4 -

2100 HOURS - ZERO DAY +6

THE CLAN MOVED north to the strip of trees that ran east-to-west, separating the occupied garage from the house. Now creeping westward among the trees, they stayed as silent as a dozen untrained people could. The light rapidly dimmed as they approached the western edge of the trees.

Cassy saw Michael again give the hand signal to rally around and crept forward with the other adults. When they'd all come close, Michael said, "Okay, this is it. When I give the signal, move in a crouch as fast as the kids allow. Head straight at those closest trees across the field, while I stay in position to defend. Once you are all across, I'll move out. I have to keep this plan simple for the kids, but I know we can do this."

Cassy understood that he really meant the plan was kept simple for *everyone* since Michael was the only one with real training and experience, but she nodded anyway. Michael was pretty darn good at this stuff, for being so quiet most of the time. The speech reminded everyone of the kids and took their minds off of their own fears. Five star job, she decided.

Michael crept ahead again, sidling from cover to cover

until he was near the tree line closest to the auto body shop. He kept still for about a minute, watching, and then raised his arm to wave the clan forward. More or less all at once, the group quietly moved to the last few trees and then, as Michael had directed earlier, moved out in pairs. One adult and one child left the trees, crouched as low as they could go and still move, as fast as they could without running. Five seconds later, the next pair. And then the next.

Cassy was the next-to-last to go, leaving only Jed and of course Michael. She took two deep breaths and then rushed out. Crouching low caused a sharp spike of pain to stab through her shoulder, and she nearly cried out but stopped herself by biting her lip. She was certain she bit hard enough to draw blood. The ground was uneven, and she recognized the tell-tale signs of a farm field left fallow. Once she stumbled to her knees, but with a hiss of breath from the pain, she was able to rise up again and continue. She glanced over her shoulder and saw Jed leaving the trees, the last of the clan besides Michael. So far, whoever was guarding the garage to the south and the house to the north had not noticed them, and she prayed their luck continued. Cassy saw that the first of the group to leave the trees was almost to the opposite tree line, almost safe. Cassy was still some 150 yards from safety, however. She put her head down, focusing on the terrain and on putting one foot in front of the other despite the pain in her shoulder.

Their luck was not to last. As the second adult reached the safety of the trees, a shot rang out from the south. A second later came another shot, quickly followed by one from the north. Cassy remembered what Michael had said and simply kept running, no longer bothering to crouch. Every time her foot came down the pain spiked again, and soon she saw spots and realized she was very near to passing out. If she did, her only hope would be that Michael made it out and somehow rescued her. She risked stopping for a few seconds to let the rising pain subside. It was either stop or pass out.

Jed and crew ran past her. He stopped and turned back to help while the two children kept running, but Cassy waved him on. He nodded once and was gone. That Jed was a no-bullshit guy, redneck as they come and had his share of "character defects," but his heart was good. In his world, Cassy thought, if an adult said to go on then that's what he'd do—Cassy was a grown woman and could make her own decisions. Cassy spared a smile.

Clods of dirt exploded into the air all around her as bullets struck nearby. Fuck and damn! Those bastards had seen her. Of *course* they had, she realized. She must have been the one they saw, and here she was standing still. She bolted from her spot, with adrenaline narrowing her vision; she didn't see the stone that tripped her, but suddenly she was on her face in the dirt. The fall knocked the wind out of her. Gasping for air, she frantically spun over onto her back and looked around. Muzzle flashes could be seen to either side as the people in those buildings fired, mostly at her. Where the fuck was Michael? Oh God, he must have been hit. There was no other explanation for why he wasn't returning fire from his position in the trees.

Cassy realized with sudden calm and clarity that she was about to die. Even firing in the dusk light, they would eventually hit her and then it would all be over. She couldn't crawl because of her shoulder, and if she tried to get up to run they would only have a better target. She lay back and waited with eyes closed, resigned to her fate, and prayed once again to thank whatever god existed that her children had already made it to the far trees. At least she had the foresight to tell Frank how to get to her homestead. The clan would make it. Her children would make it home.

A bright light shone through her closed eyelids. Confused, she opened her eyes to look around. To the south, where the garage had been, there was now only a mushroom cloud of fire and smoke. She heard screams in the distance, but within seconds, they stopped. The muzzle flashes from the northern house petered out and then stopped altogether.

Thank you, God… Fighting the pain, Cassy rose to her feet still gasping for air and stumbled toward the tree line and safety. It was slow going with the wind still knocked out of her, but she pushed herself as hard as she could.

There was a sound to her left. Cassy fearfully turned her head to look but realized with a start that the noise came from Michael, who was sprinting toward her. He skidded to a stop when he reached her and without a word grabbed her around the waist with his left arm. He half helped, half dragged her toward the trees.

Moving as fast as she was able, they quickly reached the tree line but kept going until they were some fifty yards into the woods. The rest of the clan followed along in silence until Michael stopped to gently help Cassy to the leaf-littered ground.

* * *

2115 HOURS - ZERO DAY +6

Frank took stock of the situation. Michael had used only a half dozen rounds and was the only one who had fired. That irritated Frank on principle, but he reminded himself that those were Michael's instructions. Well, Michael knew how to do this stuff better than anyone else, but it still left a sour taste that he'd been unable to really contribute during the riskiest parts. He was sure he could have helped.

But his initial irritation was overshadowed by the fact

that no one following Michael's plan had been seriously hurt. Jed had fallen into the tree line when a bullet grazed his leg and had a bruised knee that made him limp slightly, but the graze itself was easily bandaged. Cassy's ankle wasn't sprained, thankfully—she'd suffered enough lately without that, and they didn't need her moving any slower than she already did. Nor had her shoulder opened up again when she fell. All good. Most of the kids had started to cry out of fear when they got to the safety of the trees, but none had frozen in place out in the open when the shooting started. Again, all good.

Michael finished his check of everyone in the group and sat next to Frank with a grunt.

"Well, your plan worked, Michael. We owe you our lives. Those assholes opened fire without so much as a warning. I hope you killed them all." Frank's jaw clenched, and he wished he could go back and kill every damn last one of those bastards again, plus any Michael had missed.

Michael frowned, and his eyebrows furrowed as he stared at Frank. "No, Frank, I did not. I killed who I had to, and no more. Fact is, we all made it only because the garage had a huge propane tank at the back of the building. Must have been grandfathered in or done without permits, because it sure wasn't to code. I blew the shit out of that fucker, but propane burns in a flash without so much heat. Even people in the blast could have survived if they weren't shredded by shrapnel from the tank or from the cinder block wall. But it gave them something more important to worry about than us."

Frank didn't flinch from Michael's gaze. "That's too bad. They shot at my people, and I wish we'd been able to do more to them. Like slit every damn one of their throats and watch the light leave their eyes as they died. They shot at kids, and they deserved more than they got."

Michael slowly shook his head, disapproving. "Frank, they're civilians. They are scared of people taking what little they have, and they probably haven't eaten more than a candy bar in days, with no light at the end of that tunnel. They were doing exactly what we are—taking care of their own, as best they can. If your kid was starving, I'd kill anyone I could just on the chance they had something for your kid to eat. Same for the rest of us. Frank, someday you'll understand that we aren't any better than them. Just luckier."

Frank finally looked away from Michael's iron gaze and stared at the ground in front of him. Michael's words made sense, and Frank tried to reconcile himself to what his friend had said. But deep inside, he just knew Michael was wrong. We *are* better than them, he insisted and tried to convince himself that he would never do what Michael had said, no matter what. Deep inside, though, he worried that Michael was right, and hated himself for admitting it.

- 5 -

2130 HOURS - ZERO DAY +6

SWEATING FROM THE pace, Jaz was relieved when Michael finally said they were far enough away to rest safely for a time. In the days since the lights went out, she had done so much walking and running, not to mention carrying a heavy backpack, that she had lost several pounds. Better yet, it was all fat; her muscles were getting more toned. But the blisters on her feet were gross. She had found better shoes, but they were *so* not pretty. Blisters and ugly shoes, OMG, it *wasn't her*. It wasn't.

Jaz looked around the group, thankful that everyone had made it through the little skirmish. She saw Cassy sitting with Michael and his wife, no doubt talking about prepper stuff as usual. Cassy wasn't exactly friendly yet, but at least now she didn't feel like Cassy wanted to cut her throat while she slept. And she only took a backpack from Cassy. So build a bridge and get over it, already.

Jed's wife Amber was talking to Ethan. Well, Jaz had been around long enough to know what was going on there, even if Jed and Ethan didn't. Men. They all wanted it, and none of them had a clue. Amber was bored of Jed and ready to get into Ethan. Men were dumb and never seemed to know when a girl was into them even if she made it totally obvious. But that was cool—let the two of them talk. That left Jed sitting off to the side by himself, which suited Jaz just fine.

Jaz plopped down beside Jed, her arm brushing against his, and he turned to smile at her. "Heya girlie, how you doin'?" His eyes briefly roamed over her before locking with her own eyes.

A thrill went through her then. Men almost always did that, unless they were gay—her gay friends never did that unless it was to check out her outfit—and she usually didn't even notice anymore. It was just what men did. But when Jed looked at her, she felt her heart beat just a little faster. It had been awhile since any guy got a rise out of her, she suddenly realized. Maybe something was wrong with her.

"I'm okay," she told Jed. "Like, not totally okay because you scared the shit out of me out there when the bullets started buzzing around, but I'm holding up." She looked into his eyes, his blue eyes that sorta swallowed her up, and counted to three before looking away with a smile. That was being coy, her mom had taught her. It often worked. "I thought you got shot," she added, putting a little wobble into her voice.

"Oh, and that worried you, did it? Best be careful, or a man will get to thinkin' you like him or something."

Again with that smile of his. And it seemed to drown out all her worries, all her bad memories, and hidden secrets. Maybe she really did like him. Yeah, the more she thought about it, the more she thought maybe she "like liked" him. But he was married...

"Of course I like you, Jed. You're strong and good, and rough around the edges. You're, like, a good friend maybe. I hope you are. But you know you have other responsibilities. I don't know if Amber is okay with you having a friend like me."

Jed looked far away and was silent for a long moment. Finally, he said, "Jaz, me 'n Amber haven't been what you call 'close' in years. Not since we lost our other son, drowned in the crick. She blames me. I reckon she stays with my sorry ass out of love for the kids. She surely does love them, you know. But I seen how she looks at Ethan. Same as she used to look at me before I asked her out the first time. And he's a good man, that Ethan. I think we'll all be in this together for longer than we might think, and I reckon I don't much worry about what she and Ethan do together down the road. But right now isn't the time and not all secretive and sneaky when they do. I hope."

Jaz froze. Oh God, he'd never opened up like that before, not in any of their sometimes long talks along the way. The guy was hurt, but *still* only wanted Amber to be happy! She'd have to seriously reconsider this guy. Maybe he wasn't so rough around the edges after all. And Jed said he and Amber had been distant for years. Long enough for him to come to grips with it. No need for rebounding, maybe. Oh, what the hell was she thinking? Did she really like him like *that*?

"Jed, it like, hurts me to hear that. She's a good person, but so are you. I think both of you should have a chance to be happy. If you're okay with her kicking it with Ethan, maybe she'll, like, be okay with us being friends? I kinda think maybe we could be... really close friends. I want to be."

Jed slid an arm around her waist, and she rested her head on his shoulder. Jed let out a long, deep breath. "Jaz, you got more in your head than just friends, I think. I been thinkin' about that too, for a while now. I haven't smiled a real smile in a long, long time before you came along. I like being around you, girlie. You make me smile again. Let's ease into it and see how Amber deals with us being friends. Okay?"

With that, Jed stood and strode over to Michael and Cassy without a look back. Jaz had an avalanche of thoughts all tumbling around in her head, and she stared into the trees, thinking. Then she glanced around when she realized she'd spaced out. Jed and Michael were talking about something or other, but not Cassy. Sitting by Michael, Cassy stared at Jaz with one eyebrow half-raised, and she felt her cheeks flush red. Cassy made one curt nod and then turned away to Michael and Jed's conversation.

Jaz was once more alone with her thoughts, wondering what Cassy meant when she nodded at her like that.

* * *

Just before the sun went down completely, Cassy and the others finished preparing the make-shift encampment; latrine dug, coals burning merrily, and wool blankets set up as lean-tos around the fire, with another wool blanket under each lean-to set atop a bed of leaves and needles to insulate them from the ground. Sleeping in the rough with comfort, Cassy smiled to herself.

To the south was the town of Devault; occasional gunshots could be heard from there, faint reports carried on the wind. Cassy and the others had already been briefed for the next day's run because Michael insisted everyone know the plan just in case they had to flee during the night. Everyone could meet up at the next day's encampment spot, if necessary, even if they split up and traveled alone. In the morning, they would travel along the I-76 greenbelt to the west until it ran out in a few miles, then bypass the town of Eagle by diverting north, and then, by the end of tomorrow, they should be in a thick greenbelt west of the little village of

Ludwig's Corner.

Cassy sat next to her mother, staying quiet for several minutes. She enjoyed Mandy's company, but at the moment she was just glad her mom, along with her kids, had survived long enough for Cassy to meet back up with them. Things had gotten dicey a few times on her way back.

Mandy shifted and looked at Cassy. "So what's on your mind, sweetie? I know when you're thinking about something bothersome."

Cassy pursed her lips and nodded once. "Yeah. Well, I want your advice. I am worried about a situation that might blow up on us down the road, and I'm letting my own feelings get in the way of my judgment, I can feel it happening." She paused and added, "I know I can trust you not to be a gossip. It bothers me that Jaz and Jed are getting closer than they ought to, him being married and all. But Jed's wife Amber is spending more time than she ought to with Ethan. It's hard to feel bad for her about Jed when she's doing the same thing with Ethan. It feels like a soap opera without any commercials for going to the bathroom. Should I even bring it up? Leave it alone? I don't know what's best, Mom."

Mandy was quiet for a minute, and Cassy saw her brow furrow. Her mom always did that when she was working through a tough moral issue in her mind. Finally, Mandy said, "Well, Jed and Amber had problems before all this started, I gather. Seems reasonable they'd have even more now. Ethan and Jaz are both single and scared like the rest of us. Everyone wants someone to comfort them, I think. And I think that if Amber makes a move on Ethan before Jaz moves on Jed, all will be well."

She looked over at her daughter and added, "The world is different now, and people want different things than they did when they could distract themselves with TV and the

Internet. There's nothing wrong with people realigning themselves, and God will forgive 'em if they handle it with honor and honesty. That's all I can really say about that, sweetie."

Cassy stared into the burning coals in the fire pit. Maybe her mother was right. It was a new way of looking at things. The trick would be to see whether Amber stepped out on her marriage before Jed did, and the best way to make sure it happened that way was to try to keep Jaz away from Jed, at least for now. Running for their lives was not the right time for all this to happen anyway.

When Mandy rose to attend to the kids, Cassy didn't even notice, lost in her own thoughts again.

* * *

1800 HOURS - ZERO DAY +7

Cassy stopped with the others at the day's destination and immediately took another Percocet, chewing it to get faster pain relief. Her shoulder throbbed constantly now, and for the last mile or two, every step had driven a sharp, fiery stake through her injured shoulder joint. It had been all she could do not to cry out, and now she was pale and noticeably shaking.

At least they were done walking for the day. The sun would set in an hour, according to Ethan, and they had made it without incident to their designated stop point, an area of thick foliage just west of a village called Ludwig's Corner. Along the way, they had seen burning houses, and bodies sprawled here and there almost always showing evidence of a violent death. Michael had said those were just the tip of the iceberg. The corpses they couldn't see, tucked away in houses and in looted stores, probably vastly outnumbered the few bodies they had noticed. It bothered Cassy that she seemed to be getting used to the bodies of strangers.

Twice they had been approached by small groups of people who Cassy thought looked like families, who'd begged them for food or water. The Clan was well-armed, and the families had left without violence when Michael ordered them away. His military bark probably would have kept those timid souls away even without the guns, Cassy thought, but to hell with taking chances. Any one of them might have slipped a knife into their throats for food, Cassy figured, so she had no moral problem with the others pointing guns at the beggars.

"Well," Ethan said as he and Michael began the process of organizing an encampment, "I think pretty soon the only ones left will be farmers and people with guns, like us."

"But, don't you think the railroads still work?" Grandma Mandy asked. "The engines don't use electricity, right? They'll be rolling food out from Iowa or wherever, real soon."

Cassy thought Mandy sounded more hopeful than certain. "Mom, the trains may run on diesel, but they have computers and circuits to control everything. They're as fried as the rest of the grid. And without working trucks to get the food to the railways, how would the trains load and unload anyway? We're on our own."

Ethan grunted. "The sooner we get used to the idea that this is going to get much worse before it gets better, the safer we'll be. And don't forget about the invaders. They're attacking through Alaska, Florida, and as we know, New York. There may be other places as well. Nothing gets better until they're kicked the fuck off U.S. soil."

Michael grinned and said, "Yeah, but every damn American has a gun, practically. I bet good ol' boys are harassing them every time they step outside."

"Well, let's hope so," Cassy said. "The more soldiers who

get tied up in New York, the better off we'll be in Pennsylvania. And, unfortunately, the faster people starve off, the safer we'll be on my farm when we get there."

Cassy saw Mandy staring at her with her jaw open in disbelief. She couldn't look her mom in the eyes so she turned away to string up her shelter for the night. She heard Michael tell Mandy, "Don't look at her like that. She's being practical. You want your grandkids to live long enough to have families of their own? You better get practical, too."

Mandy spun on her heels and strode away, but not before Cassy heard her mutter, "God will punish the cruel and wicked."

Cassy hoped she was right, but she had in mind a different set of cruel people. "Save God's wrath for the invaders, Mom," she called after Mandy. To herself, she added, "They're the ones who did this to us. If there's a God, then He will know."

Ethan shook his head. "God's not in right now. Can I take a message?"

* * *

Peter Ixin fumed in his camp. For the last half-hour, he had kept his prey in his rifle sight, rehearsing in his mind the look she would have on her face when death came for her as his bullet pierced her icy heart. He prayed she would live just long enough to realize her end had come. It took all of his will not to shoot her then and there, a second-by-second struggle between his head and his heart.

But no, now was not the time. She had to live long enough to lead her group of refugees to wherever they were going. They clearly had a destination in mind, and by God, Peter would see where it was and then lead his own people there to take it. His people deserved it, and the spy and her cronies deserved nothing. There would be no mercy, Peter decided, when it came time to take out the trash.

Peter slid his aim to the spy's left. There was the muscle man, who had to be a soldier of some sort. He was always on point and had been their scout every time they moved out. Maybe it would be worth it to take him out right now. Of the group, he seemed the only real threat to Peter's own men when they came a' callin'. He slid his finger from the rifle's upper receiver to the trigger, and calculated wind and distance, quickly doing the math. With his other hand, he clicked his scope's dials, one click for windage, two for distance. That ought to do it...

Then it occurred to Peter that the refugees might not make it to their base, or wherever they were headed, without Muscle Guy's help. He weighed the pros and cons of just wasting the bastard right there and then. His finger rested lightly on the trigger as he weighed the options in his mind. Jaw clenched, he took two deep breaths and then held his breath mid-exhale.

And made his decision.

- 6 -

1830 HOURS - ZERO DAY +7

CASSY CARRIED AN armful of kindling and getting it had hurt like a bitch. She had to gather it on the ground first, stack it so that all the wood lay in the same direction, and then scoot down to try to get an armful. What a pain in the ass. Still, she thought, there was no way she was going to let herself be useless until her shoulder healed, whenever that would be. Though it might take forever to gather kindling up in this way, she would otherwise be doing nothing at all.

She bent over to drop the kindling onto her growing pile of wood and slammed her arm into a branch of the tree that sheltered the wood and the fire pit. She let out a scream of pain and then fell to her knees, clenching her eyes shut and gritting her teeth.

She felt a hand drop on her left shoulder, the good one, and lightly rub her arm, her back, her shoulder. When the pain subsided enough to speak, Cassy looked up. It was Jaz who had stopped to help her. Cassy didn't quite know how to feel about that. Her smile turned to a blank expression, and she froze. "Jaz. Thank you," she said, but her expression didn't change.

Jaz didn't reply but bent over to grip Cassy's good elbow and lifted. It hurt, but Cassy rose with her. Getting up with one good arm had been a problem, but apparently Jaz had noticed. So what the hell was that little thief doing helping her, Cassy thought, and why now?

"Cassy," said Jaz, unable to meet Cassy's eyes, "can we like, talk or something? Just you and me? I need to say some things, and you might want to hear what I have to say."

Cassy fought the urge to roll her eyes. Jaz was pretty and dumb. Pretty dumb. At least that's all she'd shown of herself so far, as far as Cassy was concerned. "Sure. I need to sit down, though. Over there," she said and pointed to a nearby log. It was far enough away for privacy, but close enough that Cassy wouldn't suffer in getting to it.

They walked to the log, Jaz hovering around Cassy apparently ready in case Cassy fell, and the two sat down together.

"What do you want, Jaz? You know how I feel about you, or at least some of it."

Jaz looked at the ground, then back up at Cassy. "So tell me how you feel about me, Cassy. All of it. I have some things to say, and it's easier if I know, like, the whole story."

"Fine. You pretended to be friendly and stole my supplies. I could have died out there. Then you pretended to be friendly to the clan and nearly got them all killed. Yet they still accepted you, even knowing that. You don't deserve them as friends, Jaz. And now you are moving in on Amber's husband. You're oh-for-three in my book, Jaz. The others like you because you're friendly, and pretty, and nice to have around. But I *don't* like you because you *use that* to your advantage, and all you seem to do is stab people in the back." Cassy stopped and stared at Jaz.

The young woman seemed to expect Cassy to continue,

but after a long awkward silence, Jaz let out a deep sigh and looked down at her hands. "I can see where you're coming from, Cassy. Like, if I didn't know me I might think the same, so I can't blame you. But there's more to this, and you aren't giving me any bennies of the doubts." Jaz stopped and seemed to be considering what to say next.

Cassy was content to sit in silence. She'd said all she wished to say on the matter, even if it hurt the girl's feelings. Too bad.

Then Jaz said, "Listen, Cassy, when I took your backpack I didn't realize how bad things were going to get. It seemed harmless. The lights were supposed to come back on, right? I had nothing, and you were out on a pleasure hike, and it made me mad. It wasn't until I was, uh, detained by some local hickerbillies that I realized just how bad things could get. How bad they were already. And believe me, Cassy, things totally did get lots worse than I ever thought they could. So bad that I sometimes wouldn't have minded, you know, dying. Just to get away from it all. I'm glad I didn't die, but something like that changes people, right? So when those bastards told me to scout out Frank's group and signal when they were sleeping, I was going to do it. I was scared. But then I thought, 'What if they did it to the girls here? What if they used them the way they used me, instead of killing them?' I just, like, couldn't even imagine doing that to people. Because I finally knew how bad things could get." She paused, still staring down at her shoes. "I didn't target these people, but I could warn them. It got me away from the hickerbilllies with my life, and it saved some good people. It was the best I could do."

Cassy turned to stare at Jaz. Crap. Jaz made sense, no matter how much Cassy wanted to hate her, but there was still one other thing. "Be that as it may, young woman, I am surely not the only one to notice that you have an unhealthy interest in a married man. You can't blame that on what you went through before. It's a choice you're making right here and now."

Jaz actually smiled then, which irked Cassy. "About that... You see, like, he looked at me in *that way*, you know what I mean before I ever looked at him. And we've both been in the clan long enough to know that Amber is totally not into her man anymore. I don't think they were solid before the lights went out, they just stuck for the kids. And it's a whole different world now. They aren't right for each other. That's the reason Amber is all goo goo over Ethan. *In this world, right here, right now*, Ethan is the right match for her, just like I think Jed might be the right one for me. And me for him, and all that stuff. We just have to be legit with it, so no one gets hurt more than they have to, right?"

Jaz let out a long breath and stood. Then she continued, "Cassy, you're a good person and a good leader. I like you, and I trust your judgment, even if you don't like me. If you need anything, you just holler, okay?" Then she walked back to the encampment and started talking to Michael's wife, Tiffany.

Cassy, lost in her thoughts, didn't get up for nearly half an hour. What Jaz said was a lot like what her mom had said. Dammit. It made sense that people would reshuffle the relationship deck when the bedrock they were built on got shattered a week ago. Maybe Jaz *had* learned some hard lessons since the backpack thing. Hell, Cassy had more than a passing interest in Frank in fact, but of course she was mature enough to keep that to her damn self. "The hell I'm going to be like Jaz," she muttered.

Cassy shook her head to clear the thoughts and got up to help pass out the rations.

* * *

Ethan finished the last bite of his MRE and dropped the various bits of wrapping into the low fire burning in the center of camp. As on most evenings, the whole clan—minus those on 'guard duty'—sat more or less in a circle around the fire talking and joking, and planning the next day's travel. Lately, the routine had become a bit awkward—Jaz hovered around Jed, and Amber spent her meal splitting her attention between Jed and Ethan. Cassy and her mom, Mandy, spent their meal watching the others but so far neither had said anything about the dance going on around them. Ethan knew the two were watching and figured it was only a matter of time before one of them broke the silence.

In the meantime, knowing Cassy watched them made it awkward to spend time talking with Amber. That was a shame because Amber was a great woman, and he enjoyed spending time with her. If Jed would just make an actual move on Jasmine, Ethan figured, he could have a clear conscience when he did something real about Amber. His feelings weren't love, exactly, but Amber was beautiful and clearly interested. Ethan hadn't had a lot of women in his life over the years. More importantly, he could see that Amber was intelligent—too smart for Jed, for sure—and she had a razor-sharp wit. He enjoyed verbally sparring with her.

Most of all, it was refreshing to finally meet a woman who *understood* what all his prepping had been about. She didn't look at him askance when he explained why he lived in a bunker, or why he even had a bunker in the first place. All she'd said was that it would have been great if Jed thought ahead like he did.

Amber made her way around the circle then, to sit next to Ethan. "Speak of the devil," he said as she wiggled her way closer to him on the log "bench," keenly aware of her leg brushing against his. Too aware, in fact. It was awesome and weird at the same time.

"What's up, Dark Ryder?" she asked.

Using his hacker name was a bit of a joke to her, but she said it in a way that he felt was meant to be affectionate, not disrespectful. Just flippin' perfect, his hacker handle turning out to be his pet name.

Ethan grinned and wiggled his eyebrows at her. "Just counting the hours until I can get back online and do some good for the U.S. of A."

"You never really talk about what you do," she said, but it was more a question than a statement. An invitation.

"Sorry, girl, I can't talk about some of it. It's just better if you don't know the details. But basically, I keep communications open between survivor groups, isolated military units, and freedom fighters. And a few prepper compounds, too, though they don't really do much that's useful."

"You were useful, Ethan. Maybe you just need to be smart enough to figure out how to use them right."

"I could be more useful, you know," he said with an exaggerated wink.

Amber snickered. "You're incorrigible," she said with a grin. "Although I can't say I haven't thought about it. About you and me, I mean. You always make me smile and laugh. I don't feel so angry all the time when you're around."

"I think that may have something to do with you not being invested in your marriage anymore. You haven't been for a long time. At least, that's my reading from some of the things we've talked about."

"That may be, hon," she said, slowly shaking her head. "But Jed and I are parents, and we took vows."

"Well, I'm not saying that I want you to leave your husband, but so what if you did? The world has changed. We're a clan now, apparently. I don't think that will change regardless, so you'd still have your kid. The vows you took in the old world, it seems to me, expired when it did. Relationships don't exist in a vacuum, they exist in a context. The context of your marriage isn't what it was a week ago."

Amber sat in silence, looking pensive, and Ethan was content simply to sit by her companionably and let her think. Part of him wanted nothing more than to lean over and kiss her—just take her in his arms and let the chips fall where they may—but another part of him felt guilty for even thinking it. The world might change in a day, but people took more time. Amber was married. And yet... The old world they knew was burning, and if her marriage burned up with it, maybe that wasn't so tragic. Her kid would still have his dad. Hell, the whole clan was acting like one big, extended family with the kids, and they seemed to actually be happy about it.

He was torn from his thoughts when Amber jumped to her feet. She faced him with that oh-so-wonderful smile and said, "I need to go check on the kids. Later you can tell me about one of your silly online castle raids, okay? I love how excited you get when you talk about that stuff."

Ethan nodded and watched her walk away. Amber was in her early thirties and had a child, but her walk still looked amazing. Okay, maybe not so stunning to everyone, though she was cute by anyone's standard. But her strong inner self shone out, and she lit up his world when she smiled, which only made her more beautiful. If only she would just tell him what she wanted... Ethan turned away to stare at the fire, his emotions jumbled and conflicting.

- 7 -

1930 HOURS - ZERO DAY +7

TAGGART FIRED TWO rounds and ducked back behind the derelict subway car. The ping-ping of return fire struck the car almost immediately. There were ten enemy soldiers when the shooting started, but now only one remained. Too bad this wasn't Taggart's mission target. It was only an unpleasant surprise along the way to the real ambush.

Captain Taggart's men for the mission consisted of Pvt. Eagan, two new Resistance recruits, and two "experienced" Resistance fighters. Taggart now understood that being experienced was code for Militia members, and so he didn't trust them at all. Still, they had been obedient and disciplined so far. The Resistance was the only game in town for food, unless someone wanted to volunteer for slave labor with the enemy. Plenty of people did, despite the risks, now that the food was mostly gone.

The *crack* of a rifle signaled the end of the engagement when one of the Militia members, ordered to circle around the other side of the subway car, took off the enemy's head with his Remington 700. A damn fine hunting rifle as far as

Taggart was concerned, and today they were hunting in earnest.

"Listen up," Taggart barked. "Gather their weapons, ammo, and any radios or food they have on them, and stash it in the conductor's car. Toss these bastards into the passenger car. Eagan—don't forget our new orders to spray paint the 'Circle R' so they know who did this. We go in three mikes."

They were done in two minutes, and Taggart resisted the urge to smile at the eagerness with which these civilians followed his orders. Of course, the invaders hadn't been able to fire back much this time, having been taken by complete surprise. How his civvies would handle being shot at by enemy soldiers on the bounce remained to be seen.

Well, he'd see soon. They were only a few blocks from where they would pop up from the subway into the city above, then it would be time to set up their ambush of a supply convoy heading out of New York to go to God-knows-where.

Twenty minutes later they were above ground and in place for the Op. Taggart and a Militia guy in a second-story window; Eagan and a new recruit behind a dumpster filled with rubble; and the last Militia man and recruit in another building on the first floor. The triangulation of fire would hopefully ensure the quick demise of the convoy defenders, without confusing his own untrained men. But before the shooting would start, two sticks of dynamite in a shoe box on the roadway would stop the convoy cold once Taggart pushed the button. Hopefully.

In ten mikes the convoy should go by (according to Mr. Black's intel, which might well have come from the 20s, whoever *they* were). Taggart hated this part. As always, the waiting made it the longest ten minutes of Taggart's life, at least until the next time. The minutes ticked by, each seeming like hours, but eventually he heard the roar of engines approaching. He clicked his radio. "Heads up. OpFor inbound. Tiger One, ready."

The radio responded. "Tiger Two, ready." Then, "Tiger Three, ready."

There was a noise behind him—the scuff of shoes on linoleum. Taggart spun, bringing his M4 to bear at the same time. It took half a second to understand what he saw. Four civilians crept toward him carrying a bat, a chain, and two kitchen knives. They had hunger in their eyes, and desperation.

"Halt. Disperse immediately. This city is under Martial Law by decree of the Commander-in-Chief, and you are required to vacate the area immediately," said Taggart with his best "Sergeant's bark."

Behind him the hum of an engine was becoming a roar of multiple vehicles; the convoy was getting close. Then his radio chirped. "Captain, hostile civilians approaching, request permission to fire." That would be Eagan. As soon as the radio chirped clear, another voice called out, "Yeah, here too, Cap. Tiger Three about to be engaged by at least ten people with... knives n' shit." That would be the Militia guy.

One of the men approaching Taggart—the one with the bat—said, "I don't give a fuck about them other guys, they aren't with us. But you got food, and we're gonna get it. You can't stop all of us. Hand it over, or I'll cut off your dick and feed it to you."

Just great. The approaching engines were nearly in the target zone, too. "This is a mission, and there's supplies in that convoy. Enough for all of you. Disperse until we take it." Not that the other civvies would know if these guys agreed. He needn't have worried, however.

The man sprung forward, bat held in two hands overhead to swing it down on Taggart's skull. Abruptly two red flowers blossomed on the man's chest, and he fell onto his face, then lay still. Taggart's ears rang from his Militia companion's double-tap. He glanced over and saw the wiry man holding an H&K pistol, now pointed at the remaining three.

Outside, Taggart heard popcorn going off—the sound of the other teams being engaged, and firing. Taggart opened fire at the remaining three men. In under one second, all three were down and dying or dead. The sounds of his other teams firing echoed off the buildings and faded; they too were now either dead or victorious.

The Militia man turned to Taggart even as he dropped the pistol and took up his hunting rifle, nodded once, and turned toward the window. Taggart jumped toward the window and flipped the switch on his small transmitter box, and was rewarded with the deep *boom* of the sticks of dynamite going off. A secondary explosion told Taggart the bomb had taken out a vehicle. There was the screech of tires as the other convoy vehicles halted, and then more popcorn —the distinctive sounds of AKs—as the enemy panic-fired in all directions. A loud, clear voice called out in Arabic, and the enemy fire dwindled to nothing. Must be their commander getting his ratfuck soldiers in order.

By the time Taggart could get back up and peer over the window ledge, the enemy had stopped and dispersed. There were at least thirty of the bastards out there buzzing like hornets to every available piece of cover. Engaging them now would be suicide. Fuck and damn and every other curse word he could think of.

Taggart clicked his radio. "Abort, abort. Rally at exit B or C if you can. Good luck." He turned to his Militia companion. "Bug out time, soldier. Grab your gear and retreat," he said, more loudly than he'd intended. Adrenaline, yeah.

But his companion snarled at him, instead of moving

out. "Traitor! Kill them or die," he cried.

The man actually had tears in his eyes, Taggart noted, a damn strange thing to notice right now. Taggart was done. There was no way he could get his weapon into play before this Militia fanatic punched Taggart's ticket permanently. Taggart tried to be as calm as possible and said, "Listen, brother, go easy. We're on the same team here…"

The Militia man's chest exploded, showering the room in crimson gore. Then Taggart heard the deep thump of a heavy machine gun firing from below. Some raghead got a lucky shot in, taking the rabid Militia man out. Thank God.

Taggart grabbed his pack under his left arm and ran, leaping over the civilian bodies. He sprinted out of the apartment to the stairs and was about to leap down to the next landing when he heard glass break below, and a flurry of noise and voices. The enemy was on their way up. Taggart checked his momentum, bouncing painfully off the railing, and flew down the hallway to the unit on the end. He didn't slow down, just leapt into the air and struck the door with his right boot near the door handle, smashing it open. His momentum carried him through the doorway and into the unit. Inside, two women hiding from the window by crouching behind the couch turned toward the surprise visitor and screamed.

Taggart kept going. He brought his pack up from under his arm and held it before him as he vaulted up to the back of the couch, landing on one foot, and leapt again straight through the large window. His backpack protected him from most of the glass, though he felt a few burning slices in his arms and legs, and fell like a rock. Two stories passed in under two seconds, and he hit the ground hard. Taggart rolled as though this was a parachute landing, as he'd been taught, and came up on his feet. The adrenaline blocked the pain of any injury he may have sustained, thankfully, and he sprinted toward a nearby alley. He heard rifles firing behind him, and as he passed into the alleyway he heard the sharp sounds of bullets striking brick next to him.

And then he was out of their view. He didn't stop running. Part of him wondered whether the others had escaped, but he had no time to dwell on it. The enemy would surely be coming after him, and it was time to run for his life.

- 8 -

2000 HOURS - ZERO DAY +7

STEVEN WALLACE STUMBLED under the weight of the basket strapped to his back, which was filled with rubble. A moment later the pain of 50,000 volts of electricity struck him in the arm. With a convulsive full-body twitch he flopped forward and landed on his face, without even the ability to use his arms out to break his fall. The rubble from the basket cascaded over his head, and he heard riotous laughter nearby.

Steven's face flushed with anger, but as soon as his body would let him he rose to his knees, took off his basket, and began shoveling debris back into it. The Foreman, as the workers had named him, would sooner put a bullet into his head than wait for a slow worker. Back on his feet, Steven began the trudge once again, this time with a quicker pace.

A building had been destroyed by a missile, and Steven's group of workers was tasked with moving it from the site. Every day they had to carry a certain number of baskets half a mile north to the island's coast, where their contents were added to the growing wall of rubble the invaders were building around the city. Of the twenty-odd men who had begun the task with him three days ago, only eleven remained—but those eleven were given plenty of food and water every day that they worked. As long as he kept trudging, Steven's family got to eat.

He had to remind himself of that fact, chanting it in his mind over and over. It was the only way to keep going, and to ignore the growing string of heads stuck on poles and fences along the route between the building site and the rubble wall. The heads were the invaders' way of warning the remaining workers not to slack off or fall out. Steven was tired, but at least he wasn't a head on a stick yet. Last week Steven was an accountant, but that life seemed very distant already.

Ahead of him, a short and wiry young man staggered to his knees. Steven had thought the man would break on the first day, but somehow he had kept up while others dropped out.

"Get up, Mark," Steven urged in a half-whisper.

"I'm trying," said the young man. He looked at Steven, and there were tears streaming down his face. "I can't make my legs move anymore!"

"They'll fucking kill you, Mark. Get up and your family eats."

The Foreman noticed the delay. He turned and strode toward the man with a sneer on his face.

"Goddammit, Mark, the Foreman's coming. Get up!"

Mark groaned and struggled to rise to his feet. The heavy basket creaked as the rocks within shifted around. He got one foot under him and tried to rise, legs quaking, but the man's tired, abused muscles wouldn't do it. His leg gave out, and he fell to the ground on his side.

The Foreman arrived, and Steven shut up. One did not talk while the Foreman was around. The soldier had short hair and a long beard and wore a black shemagh around his neck, which matched the black fatigues he wore. "What are you doing? Get up, son of bitch."

Steven watched as Mark turned his head to look at the Foreman. Tears running down his face, Mark cried out, "I can't move anymore! God, please, just give me five minutes. I swear I'll get up in five minutes."

Steven flinched at the raw terror in Mark's voice and eyes that were wide with fear, and at the Foreman's sneer. The son of a bitch looked happy, and that meant only one thing.

"God will not help you. Allahu akbar! Get up or face justice."

Mark didn't move. Steven watched in mute horror as the Foreman pulled a large knife from a sheath on his belt, knelt down and grabbed Mark's hair, and pulled the victim's head back to expose his throat. Mark screamed in terror, an inhuman sound that Steven had heard nine times before. The Foreman paid no attention, however, and seemed not even to hear Mark's cries. With one smooth motion, he drew the wicked knife across Mark's throat, and a spray of blood splattered into the dirt.

Of course, thought Steven, none of it hit the Foreman. That bastard made sure he was behind his victim, so the blood sprayed away from him.

Then the Foreman shoved Mark forward, face down into the bloody dirt. As he did so, he wore a smile, a happy fucking smile, and muttered his "Allahu akbars" over and over. Steven wished he had the courage to kill that smiling, evil bastard. But that would be suicide, and so Steven stood mutely and looked away from the familiar scene.

Like clockwork, the Foreman waited ten seconds after Mark stopped twitching in the bloody mud, then leaned down again to finish his grisly work. In short order, it was all over, and the soldier stood with Mark's head in his hand, held by the hair, and raised it to the sky with a great cry of victory. Steven didn't know what he was saying, but it sounded like the same thing every time this scene had repeated itself.

The Foreman walked over to a wrought iron fence and gently, almost reverently slid one iron spike up into the head through the grisly neck. Then he turned and faced the remaining workers.

"Ten of you remain. Do not be lazy! You have duty to job. Soft Americans, you must work harder now. Half you failed Allah's test, and rest of you son of bitch must do twice the work. Say prayer to Allah for this man, and get back to work."

The Foreman turned and spit on Mark's impaled head, but the workers who remained only resumed the long walk to the rubble wall.

Maybe they'd get more slaves to join them soon. For the love of God, let there be more slaves soon, he thought. If they didn't get more people to help, there was no way he could keep up the pace much longer.

* * *

Luis "Spyder" Acosta was king of his world, now. Three blocks along West Cumberland and North 33rd were now indisputably his. Luis and his crew had fought or absorbed every other crew in the neighborhood, and now his gang owned it all. It was hard to get drugs now, but his bitches were raking in a fortune—all in trade for food, bullets, anything useful. He had his street-level guys herding the sheep people, which was anyone not in his gang, building a barrier around his turf with abandoned cars and rubble. Once they were done, he would start gobbling up blocks one at a time, walling them up, and moving on to the next block.

Soon his dream of becoming "King Spyder" could become a reality.

That was, of course, if the damn invaders let him. He was never sure whether they'd allow something until he tried it. If they didn't care, then the food kept coming. If they didn't like it, though, it would be a hungry couple of days; they'd said they would not deliver food for several days every time someone in his crew screwed up.

So far raping, beating, and even killing people had not upset the ragheads. As long as his crew lit up anyone with a gun, turned over or killed anyone wearing a U.S. military uniform, and delivered two slaves a day, the invaders left him alone. Those two slaves were easy to catch from the turf of that puto, Angel, a block south. Angel's block would be the first to go, Spyder decided. That dumb son of a bitch wasn't even building a wall.

Better yet, because of the deal he'd brokered with them, the invaders would deliver two or three days of food for his neighborhood three times weekly, and drop it off practically at his doorstep. If the losers who lived in Spyder's territory wanted to eat, they better cough up something he wanted. The women had it easy, at least if they were young and hot, and even if he wasn't in the mood to get laid then he could pass 'em off to his crew to keep them loyal. Them ugly bitches could trade like all them dudes had to. And Spyder wasn't no racist, neither—anyone who could trade work or goods would eat under Spyder's rule, hell yeah. Keep them hungry, but fed, and they'd be too fucking afraid to fight back.

The only real challenge for him, as far as keeping the invaders happy, was all the damn "Resistance" fighters running around. Every time they raided the invaders, the ragheads got all riled up. And that was just one more reason to take Angel's territory because that weak-ass brotha wasn't able to fight off the Resistance. Rumor had it that Angel's turf was crawling with Resistance putos. Well, hopefully not for long...

There was a knock at Spyder's door, and then Sebastian walked in. Big, dumb, and mean, Sebastian was a good lieutenant, but he never waited to come inside after knocking.

"What is it," Luis snapped.

"Spyder, we got the first stuff from the ragheads. I had the boys make some peeps carry it into the lobby downstairs like you said. But, there's a problem."

Luis waited for Sebastian to continue, but the dumb fuck just stared back. "Great, Seb. So, tell me, what the hell is the problem?"

Sebastian nodded, oblivious to his boss's irritation. "Well, there's like twenty peeps outside, demanding food. They got knives and bats n' shit."

"Listen, Sebastian... You're my main guy, right? Because you know how to bust heads and keep peeps and the crew in order. So, go bust some fuckin' heads. Feel free to shoot a couple, if you want. Use as many of our boys as you need to get the job done. I want these putos to remember that I'm in charge. This is Spyder's territory, and they all belong to me. Make the survivors remember that, Seb. Tell the crew to have some fun with it."

Luis watched Sebastian grin and then leave without another word. Yeah, Seb was a big, dumb animal, but a useful one. And loyal as anyone could be since Luis saved his life, and then did two years in the pen rather than rat Seb out to the cops. Hell, if he had ten more guys like Sebastian, he wouldn't need any of the others at all.

There was another knock at the door. "What the hell do you want," he snapped, and the door opened. It was Charlene, who was one fine piece of ass. Spyder had tried to get with her a while back, but she was uppity back then because she had gotten some two-year degree somewhere. Fat lot of good it did the bitch now. "I said, what the hell do you want, bitch?"

Charlene looked at the floor to avoid Luis's eyes. Smart bitch.

"Spyder, I'm sorry I said no, before. I was hoping, like, you might like to put it down, because I'm so damn hungry. And I know you don't hold grudges, and stuff, so..."

So. Char wanted to trade a piece of that fine ass for a meal. Served the bitch right for turning him down before. Oh yes, he would trade, but when he put it down on her, she was gonna walk wrong for a week. Teach her a lesson about manners when she talked to him, Spyder, King of the neighborhood.

"Yeah, girl. Show me what you got, first, and then you know what I want. I'ma make your eyes water before I put it down with you, and none of that fake choking noise bullshit. Just take what I give, and then you can have some food." Life was good, Luis thought. Maybe he'd actually give her some food later if she was a good lay. "Damn, it's good to be a gangsta..."

- 9 -

2000 HOURS - ZERO DAY +7

FRANK SAT WITH his wife Mary, talking about the clan, plans, and journey. As they finished off the last of their meal, Frank thought about how much Mary hated MREs and smiled. Not much of a meal, those MREs, but at least they had calories. Mary's round, ruby cheeks flushed even redder when he smiled, a trait Frank found utterly charming.

"Oh, you think watching me eat this crap is funny, do you?" she asked, fists on her hips and brows furrowed, but the sparkle in her eye and slight upturn at the corners of her plump lips told him she was only being playful.

"Well, there's no TV here. I got a twenty dollar bet with Jed that you're going to ralph up an MRE one of these times, and I gotta watch to be sure I get my money. You know how Jed is with a bet!"

Mary laughed and punched Frank in the arm. "Well, if you win that bet you're buying me a double-shot tall Irish Cream mocha. You better, mister, because I may not be able to kick your butt, but you have to sleep sometime!"

"Maybe if you let me, you know, do stuff to you, I'd roll

over and fall asleep, and then you could steal the twenty from me." Frank wiggled his eyebrows at Mary with an over-the-top wink.

"Ha! You wish. Give me the twenty and *maybe* I'd let you do your gross guy stuff to me."

The sounds of gagging and retching came from behind them. Frank looked back and saw their son Hunter pretending to gag himself with one finger. "Ew, gross! I need bleach for my ears. Quick, who knows a good therapist? Grownups are weird!"

Frank pursed his lips, and one side of his mouth turned up into a smirk. "Yeah right, son. You think I don't see you watching all those Disney shows with cute girls in them? Someday soon, you'll *wish* you could do gross grownup stuff."

Mary playfully punched him again. "That is *so* inappropriate. I swear, sometimes it's like I'm raising two boys. No matter the age, man or boy, there's no difference."

The sounds of two kids arguing broke the moment, and with a heavy sigh, Mary got up to track down the squabblers. She walked only about ten feet away before Frank saw her suddenly look down, and freeze. Her whole body stiffened, and he heard her whimper.

"What's wrong, Mary..." he began but was cut off when his wife let out a terrible shriek of fear and pain. As he bolted to his feet, she leapt away from where she had been standing. She got some fifteen feet away, then stopped and turned, still shrieking.

Michael leapt to his feet and sprinted to where Mary had been standing even as Frank and Cassy ran to Mary's side. Cassy got there first and put her hands on Mary's shoulders.

"What's wrong," Cassy shouted over the din of Mary's cries, just as Frank arrived at his wife's side.

"Sn... Snake bite," was all he could understand through

her tears and whimpers.

"Get my knife!" Frank shouted at his son, who ran off toward their shared bedding.

"No," said Cassy, face red with adrenaline. "And no damn tourniquets!"

Frank was stunned and confused, and froze. That was his wife, and she'd just been bitten, and Cassy wouldn't let him help her. Anger rose up, but Cassy just continued talking in that forceful "mommy voice."

"Mary, sit against that tree, right now. Calm. Relax. Frank, get me a flashlight."

When Frank returned with his little Stinger mini-flashlight, Mary was sitting with her back against a tree, and Cassy was looking at something on his wife's leg with her lips pursed, jaw clenched, brows furrowed. He handed the woman his flashlight, and she examined Mary's leg again.

"Does it feel like fire running through your leg? Not like getting poked, but like your leg is on fire?"

"It... It's starting to burn," Mary managed through her tears, but she looked only more frightened now, Frank saw.

"Good, that's one hurdle down. It wasn't a coral snake, thank God Almighty. Did you hear a rattle noise, like a buzzing?"

"No," said Mary with a new hope in her eyes, but she was still pumping adrenaline. Frank thought she looked ready to lose her mind.

"It could still be a rattlesnake, but no buzzing noise is a good sign," said Cassy in a calm but friendly voice—the same voice Mary used when their son got really hurt but had to be kept calm to examine his ouchie.

Cassy then used the mini-flashlight on Mary, shining the light into both eyes for several infinitely long minutes, then looked up at Frank. "No eyelid droop. We have a real good shot that it was only a copperhead snake." She looked up and said, "Michael! See if you can find the snake!"

"Aren't copperheads venomous?" squeaked Mary, and her face looked to be torn between relief and fear of the other shoe dropping any moment.

"Sure as shit, yes they are," Cassy replied, but then she smiled and glided her fingers over Mary's hair, and moved a stray lock out of her face. "But, no one dies from a copperhead bite unless you're real young or real old, or already half-dead from something else. You are healthy."

"But what happens? Will I lose my leg? Should we go to a hospital? What about my kids?"

Cassy held up both hands, palms toward Mary. "Whoa. Calm down, take a deep breath. First thing's first. Keep the bite below your heart. Sorry honey, you sleep sitting up tonight. But, no ice, no cuts, no sucking out the poison. That shit works in movies, but these days we know better, okay?"

"How do you know all this, Cassy?" asked Mary quietly. Her shoulders slumped as the tension and fear receded, and she wiped a tear from her eye.

"I've just taken a lot of classes and done a lot of studying. Woodcraft, alternative and emergency medicine, farming... Lots of stuff. And I read a lot. Snakes that live in my area seemed like a good thing to get familiar with."

Frank swept Cassy into his arms and nearly crushed her in his grateful embrace. "Thank you, Cassy," he whispered into her ear. He saw goose bumps rise up all over Cassy's neck and shoulder, but said nothing. Instead, he stepped away and kneeled next to his wife, and held her hand. Cassy grinned at the two.

Michael returned then and held the corpse of a snake in his hand. It was about two feet long and bore the distinctive hourglass pattern of a copperhead. Frank felt a sudden relief; having a venomous snake slithering around when there were kids nearby was a recipe for disaster.

Cassy nodded at Michael and mouthed the word "thanks," then said to Frank, "Listen, she's not completely out of the woods. She almost certainly won't die or lose her leg, okay? But, she will probably have some difficulty breathing and might vomit. The leg may or may not swell up depending on how much venom the copperhead used, but any swelling shouldn't be severe. Here's the important part, Frank. Someone has to check her breathing, pulse, and temperature every hour, because if she goes into shock, we'll have to risk making her lie down with her feet elevated. Shock can be fatal quickly, Frank, but the venom would make treatment dangerous. Do you know how to check her temperature and pulse? Ethan has a glass thermometer and a wind-up watch that still works."

Frank only nodded. He had a kid, so of course he knew how to check a temperature, and he'd been an athlete before his son Hunter came along. Checking his pulse was second nature to him. Thank God that wonderful woman knew what the hell to do, and how to tell what kind of snake had bit Mary. If Cassy hadn't been there, Frank would have moved heaven and earth to get his wife to the nearest hospital, in Elverson some eight miles away, even though it would have meant risking moving fast through a forest at night. That would have been a recipe for more injuries...

"Father God, thank You for sparing my wife, and for bringing Cassy into the clan when You did. And we thank You for all Your blessings, especially those we don't know about. In Jesus' name. Amen."

Mary raised her hand and lightly stroked the growing stubble on her husband's face. "I was scared to leave you and Hunter," she said. Then her eyes got that slightly squinty look she got whenever she was feeling mischievous, and Frank grinned even before she continued, "I mean, he'd starve without someone to make sure he eats, and I haven't forgotten the week you made nothing but chili when I was visiting Mom!"

Frank forced a laugh for his wife's sake, but inside he was churning. This had been such a close call, and if not for Cassy's knowledge he might have made the bite wound worse, and spent hours trudging to the nearest hospital even knowing that it was likely looted or even occupied. It could have been a calamity.

If his clan was to survive, they would have to knuckle down and make sure everyone got at least a bit of training in all their people's combined skills. It was a damn wake up call, that's what this was. The time of overly-specialized people who knew nothing about surviving without CNN and microwaves... That time was over. Possibly forever. Frank wondered whether that would ultimately be a bad thing.

* * *

Peter Ixin sat with the woman spy in his scope, dead center, but his inner struggle kept him from squeezing the trigger. As much as he wanted—no, needed—to see the bitch die, he had a responsibility to his own people. He had to keep following her and her dipshit people to find whatever it was they were moving so purposefully toward. Then, and only then, he would return to the Farms, or whatever was left of them after the invaders had attacked it, and lead his people to safety. They would wash over this bitch and her companions like a rising flood, wash out the filth, and leave the spy's refuge as a new Eden for his own people. It just *had to work*. It was like God Himself was guiding him, and he had no doubts about how this would play out. The spy would die, and he, Peter Ixin, would be a savior and the new leader of his people. They would start again, but with Peter in charge. None of the damn leftover stupidity of the ways of the "modern world." It would be bliss. But first, he had to follow her and get back to his own people...

Peter sat back down comfortably in the small wooden shelter he'd built with fallen tree limbs, boughs, and mud. He set his rifle down and then hung up his wool blanket using makeshift clamps to fix them to a thin cross-branch.

The clamps were nothing more than six-inch bits of thick twigs, cut halfway through the middle, and split along the length from center cut to about a quarter of the distance to each end. Bending the green twigs caused the cuts to separate, but when the tension was released, the cuts closed back up again to firmly grip the edge of his blanket.

He had a small Dakota fire hole going for warmth but ate his meager food cold. The smell of food cooking would travel far and could give away his presence if the wind shifted. The fire itself, however, was almost undetectable beyond a few dozen yards at most. It burned mostly underground, and only faint wisps of smoke escaped so long as he didn't put on too much wood at once. Just keeping the coals going would give him all the warmth he needed for the night.

Peter rose up again and peered through his scope at the spy's camp. There was some sort of commotion going on with the plump wife of the group's apparent leader. A minute later he saw a muscular man, who just had to be a soldier of some kind, walking into camp holding a vine. No... Not a vine. A snake, about two feet long. So, the woman must have been bitten. Good, it served the bitch right. That was God bringing a Holy Can of Whup Ass unto them. If the woman died from the bite, the enemy would be weakened, which was good. And if she lived, they'd have to travel slower for at least a couple days, even if she only got bit by a copperhead. There were only three venomous snakes in the region, and since she still seemed coherent and able to move by herself it was probably not a rattlesnake bite. Either way, this would make it easy for him to follow them, even if he lost sight of them. Hell, he might even have enough time to forage for some berries or maybe a rabbit. He'd been carrying a stupid rabbit stick all day without seeing one damn bunny.

Yes, this was just proof that God meant for Peter to triumph, to start a new world with the good people of the Farms. He would be a generous leader to his people. Peter smiled as he thought about the terror he'd see on the face of that fat bastard who had tried to confine him to his quarters. If the pig begged enough, maybe Peter would even be merciful. Mercy was a good trait in a leader, he reminded himself, so long as it was only used sparingly.

- 10 -

2100 HOURS - ZERO DAY +7

CAPTAIN TAGGART TRUDGED wearily into the safe house Mr. Black had provided. Eagan was there already but sat next to his rifle and pack. Still sweaty, he must have just arrived. Clever one, that Eagan. Taggart decided to revise his view of the soldier. Maybe he would be useful for more than carrying a rifle.

"Eagan. Glad you made it, son. Any of our civvy friends get back alive?" Taggart cocked his head to one side to show interest, even though in his exhaustion no enthusiasm could be heard in his voice. He leaned against a wall and slid down it, taking a seat to rest.

"One. The Militia guy who was with the other civvy made it. He said the rest were killed, but that he didn't think anyone was taken alive. Surprising, from green civs."

"Aff. They did better than I'd thought, but Black said they were fighting to feed their families. I imagine the deal holds if they die for the cause, but not if they get captured."

Eagan shrugged, then lay his head back against the wall and closed his eyes.

Taggart did the same. He thought about debriefing

Eagan about how he got through the desperate people who had turned the simple ambush into a total clusterfuck but decided against it. Time enough for that later. Right now they needed rest and a catnap.

The door slammed open, and Taggart heard a flurry of curses directed at no one in particular. He let out a deep sigh and fought to open his eyes. He even managed to open one of them. Through his one open, bleary eye he saw Mr. Black storming back and forth in the room, pacing. "All present and accounted for, Black. Only fifty percent casualty rate. Of course, that's also the fatality rate."

"Not really, yo. Militia Boy came in with his arm shot up. He won't be able to fight for weeks, yo. Great job, fuckers. You screwed up a simple hit. What the fuck, soulja boy? I thought you was all tough and gung-ho, 'n shit."

"The mission was going A1 until a bunch of starving civilian shits got in our way. Nice job with the intel, by the way. It would have been nice if your 20s buddies told you about that. Or maybe they knew about it and didn't say. Do you know them? No." Taggart's jaw clenched tightly. "But they did manage to get three of your so-called troops eliminated, so you know, at least they have that going for 'em."

Eagan started to snicker, but a withering look from Taggart shut him up. Mr. Black didn't seem to notice, and still paced; he was now clenching and unclenching his fists. Bad sign. Time to change the subject.

"Black, how did the other missions go tonight? What's the operational situation, now?"

That seemed to do the trick. Black stopped pacing. He put his thumb and forefinger to the bridge of his nose, eyes closed, and took three deep breaths before again looking at Taggart.

"They went well. The intel was almost entirely straight

dope. Fifteen jobs, fourteen came back clean, with only two dead. Both were volunteers, so no big deal. We got a lot from the bastards—maps, code sheets, radios, guns, food. You're Army, so this might be bad news, yo, but D.C. is all theirs now. The White House got taken early on, sorry to say. No Commander-in-Chief for you, anymore."

Taggart smiled. Just before the lights went out, they'd gotten word that POTUS was safe in some unmarked survival shelter, and most of the rest of the civvy command structure was en route to other safe spots. Taking D.C. was a pointless gesture. Enjoy the mosquitos, fuckers. Not that Taggart much cared for the current President or any of the assholes in Congress or whatever, but with them still alive there was still a chance at getting the lights on, and getting the invaders the fuck out of the U.S. of A.

"We'll make do, Black. Eagan, go radio the other safe houses and get a SITREP. Black, will you please make sure I get the maps and other intel you picked up from the OpFor? I need to get a grip on where things stand."

Black nodded. "Yeah, sure, whatever. Fuckin' maps, okay? Bullshit. But they're yours. I'll have 'em sent to your room, along with some food. You look like shit and smell worse—wash up before you come back down." Then he stormed out of the room.

Eagan opened his eyes again and looked at Taggart. "You know, taking D.C. was awesome of them. Maybe they did us a favor and wasted my Senator. I wrote him a letter once about my bank fucking me over, and he only sent back a stupid form letter."

"You're a frikkin 'Private Pyle,' you know that? You're supposed to write your congressman for that shit. Senators are like fleas. They irritate you for a while, then go away, only to be replaced by new fleas who do the same damn thing. Anyway, the Commander-in-Chief is safe. Remember the intel we got with our last order before the shit hit the fan."

"I can always hope, Cap'n. There's always hope."

Taggart chuckled and spared a weary smile for the private. "Eagan, you are one unsat shitbird, you know that?"

"Yes, sir. The captain has provided that knowledge to the private on a daily basis, sir."

"Eagan?"

"Yes, sir, Captain, sir?" replied Eagan, one side of his mouth curled up into a smirk.

"Shut the fuck up. Let's go eat and look at some maps."

Neither of them moved for another ten minutes, but eventually, hunger overpowered their weariness. Sadly, the food only turned out to be the enemy's version of MREs and were labeled in that shitty squiggle-writing they used. They were seized supplies, of course, taken during the various raids Taggart's men were undertaking. Taggart's MRE turned out to be something like a rice-and-vegetable mush.

"Eagan, what would it take to trade for your pouch?"

"Five minutes with poor Spec-4 Louis's sister."

"He's dead, he won't mind. Done. Wherever she is, she's yours for five mikes."

"Roger that, Cap."

* * *

Cassy lounged around the fire with Aidan and Brianna to the side of her. The others were haphazardly arranged around the fire as well, and there were several conversations going on at once in more hushed tones than usual. No one wanted to awaken Mary, who, despite being bitten by a copperhead snake, was fitfully sleeping with the aid of a couple pills from Ethan's stash of medical supplies.

A sudden flash of light on the horizon caught her eye, and like the others, she turned her head to look. Then there were more and more such flashes, all to the south. Seconds later a deep, almost inaudible *THUMP* noise washed over them, felt more than heard. Cassy turned to Michael with eyes wide from fear.

"Artillery," Michael said in a monotone, almost dead-sounding voice. It was the tone he had used during the gunfight when the clan tried to sneak past the garage—his military voice. "I imagine that's the invaders, finally getting deployed in force along the I-76 Highway 30 corridor. They'll be pushing on Lancaster and Harrisburg as fast as they can, to control the Susquehanna River crossings to the west. Then on to York. That means they must have already taken Wilmington, farther south in Delaware."

Cassy turned back to the display of lights that now showed all across the southern horizon. The group was silent for a long time. So many people must be dead and dying in those blasts, that very minute, and Cassy's thoughts grew morbid.

Jed finally broke the silence. "Michael, can they be stopped? I mean, will America survive? You're the military guy, tell us how this will play down."

Michael, still with that dead voice, said, "Soon they'll have everything from Washington, D.C. to Boston on the coast, and inland to Buffalo and Cleveland. At least, I don't think we can organize a real counterattack with the grid down at least until then. But Ethan said they're in Florida, too. I think they'll push up to Richmond on the coast and inland to Charlotte and Atlanta."

Cassy frowned. That was an awful lot of territory, and would wipe out America's ability to defend anything east of the Appalachians. More importantly, in the long run, it would give the enemy a vast territory that was easy to defend by land. "So, we're screwed," she spat.

Michael shrugged. "I'm just a grunt, what do I know? But

I think you're forgetting that the U.S. is more than just the East Coast. Every redneck from Roanoke to Spokane, Washington is going to be bleeding them every minute of every day—and the more rednecks they kill, the more will sign up to play modern-day Quantrill's Raiders."

Aidan was listening to Michael intently, soaking in the man's words. "What's a Quantrill?" he asked.

Cassy patted him on the head. "Not a what, but a who. Quantrill led a group of Confederate raiders during the Civil War. They say Jesse James fought alongside him."

"I know who Jesse James was." He smiled, and Cassy smiled back. Then he returned to watching the sporadic bursts of light on the horizon.

Cassy stood up and brushed off her pants. "Gotta take a potty break," she said, and walked to the cat hole they'd dug some thirty feet into the woods. It was far enough for privacy and sanitation, but close enough to find at night without getting lost. She would have preferred it be farther into the woods, but Michael was insistent, and she eventually gave in.

Every few steps another burst of light would faintly illuminate the area, sending eerie shadows sprinting in all directions. The shadows vanished just as quickly as the light winked out. Still, she had an eerie feeling, and the hair on the back of her neck and arms stood on end. It was foolish, she knew, but she could swear someone was watching her every move.

"Is anyone there?" she asked in a hoarse near-whisper, voice starting to shake with fear. "You're psyching yourself out, girl," she told herself, but it did nothing to help abate her uneasy feeling.

Cassy reached the latrine they'd dug and unbuckled her pants. She held them up around her knees and straddled the pit as she did her best to ignore the smell. Even a fresh latrine smelled after one use, she mused, and wondered why whoever had gone before her didn't throw dirt over their mess the way she and Michael had told them.

The sound of twigs snapping to her left caught her attention. Cassy clawed at her pants to get them up and fumbled with the buckle. Her eyes never stopped scanning the area from which the noise came. After a moment, she saw a bush with long, slender leaves that looked like it was lightly swaying in the breeze, though she could feel no wind.

"Who's there?" she said in a loud, clear voice, but she couldn't help notice how shaky her voice sounded. She pulled out her pistol and racked it, putting a round in the chamber. "Show yourself, whoever it is. I don't want to hurt anyone."

As the bush continued to wave despite the lack of wind, she heard another sound to her left and spared a glance; another bush and another set of leaves moving. Whoever was out there, there were two of them. Time to go.

Cassy backed up as quickly as she could, heading toward the camp without turning her back on the moving bushes. Her pulse raced, and she felt the onset of adrenaline sweat. Her knees began to feel shaky, but she was determined not to show it. When she was close enough, she yelled for help and in seconds, she heard the welcome sounds of the clan rushing toward her and the sounds of weapons being racked. Whoever was out there wasn't going to get easy prey today.

- 11 -

2200 HOURS – ZERO DAY +7

AFTER HE AND Eagan finished eating the food they took from the invaders—disgusting mush of rice and unidentifiable green things—Capt. Taggart met with Mr. Black in a back room to go over both the most recent intel from the 20s, and the bits of information they'd either seized or coerced from the invaders during the raids earlier that day.

Mr. Black stood over the bench full of documents and notes and photographs, which itself rested under a large wall covered with maps with colored pins and handwritten notes. "So you see, jarhead…"

"That's the Marines. I'm Army."

Taggart's face was expressionless, so Black continued, "Whatever. So you see, New York is applesauce. The Invaders have everything worth having."

Taggart nodded. "We have the low-value populated areas, but only really control the areas around our safe houses and bunkers."

"The rest of those millions of people are dying now,"

Black said. "Some starving, but more getting killed by their neighbors 'n shit. Especially by that wetback, Spyder, who controls the shit just to our north, 'cause he's working with the invaders or so I hear. And the 'vaders are taking slaves from all over New York just as fast as they can round them up, with most being moved to somewhere outside of the City. We don't know where they're going, where the enemy is, or where Uncle Sam's Best are because we haven't had an update worth a shit from the 20s in days."

Taggart shrugged. "They said something about a break in the chain of communications. One of their key operatives went dark, but they hope he comes back online soon. I worry about taking help from these 20s. We know nothing about them, except that we don't have any choice but to use the intel they send us because it's better than nothing."

"Shit, you don't know what you don't know. Take your 411 when you can, not when you want it, yo."

Taggart froze but carefully kept his face expressionless. Long practice doing that when talking to officers who had their heads up their ass had made him a master at that. Of course, he was now the officer and usually felt like he had his head up his ass. He didn't know what he was doing, but all the tea in China couldn't keep him from fighting for his country and, more importantly, fighting for his boys and girls under his command. They were his.

"What did you say, Black?" asked Taggart, still expressionless.

"I said take your 411 when you get it, not when you want it. It's a thing I say when my crew don't know what they're doing and don't want to listen. Or did say, before all this shit happened."

Pvt. Eagan walked in, then. He practically skidded to a halt and looked back and forth between Taggart, rigid and frozen, and Black, who was laughing about something.

"Captain, we need you out here a minute, sir," Eagan said in a rapid-fire of words.

Taggart gave him one curt nod and followed Eagan out without saying a word to Black, who only shrugged and went back to looking at his maps. Piece of dog crap, pretending to be El Jeffe, as far as Taggart was concerned.

"What do you need, Eagan," Taggart demanded, eyes narrow and jaw clenched.

Eagan saluted. "Sir! When I entered, I think I know the captain well enough to see that he was about to rearrange Mr. Black's face, or worse. I know the captain well enough to read that body language. I felt it was my responsibility to my captain to remove him from the situation before a strategic mistake was made. Sir."

Taggart was motionless for half a minute, staring at Eagan and trying to regain full control of himself. The impertinent shit was right, dammit. Taggart had been about to tear Black apart. Finally, he let out a long, tense breath and returned the salute, releasing Eagan from his rigid position.

"Very good, Eagan. You did not read the situation wrong, I suppose, and it isn't your fault so I won't take it out on you. So. Situation report. What brought you in there in the first place?"

"What? Oh. Coffee's made, if you want a cup of November Juliet, sir. What had you so riled up? Oops, officers don't get riled up. What had the captain prepared to engage his civilian Liaison to the Resistance, in Resistance headquarters, surrounded by Resistance members?"

Taggart smiled. "You're still a shitbird, Eagan," he chuckled. "Well, the fact is, I just realized I know that guy. Mr. Black. That's not his name, of course, but before all this he was a low-level drug dealer and pimp who made most of his money running a crew of robbers. It doesn't matter how I met him, Eagan, but don't turn your back on that piece of shit. We may need his Resistance, but Mr. Black is everything we hate about civilians, thugs, all the shit wrong with the society we used to have. Don't let him charm you, Eagan. And watch my back."

Taggart stalked away still clenching his jaw, leaving a confused and worried Pvt. Eagan in his wake. He barreled through the rooms of the building, ignoring the questioning looks of both his other men and Resistance fighters, and only slowed down when he reached his quarters. He went inside, closed the door quietly, and sat on his bunk.

Thoughts raced through his mind. He couldn't fathom how a low-level gangbanger got to be the head of the local Resistance. Worse yet, how many of his crew—or worse, other crews from his gang—were here posing as righteous freedom fighters? Obviously, Black couldn't be trusted, nor could any of his men who might have been running on the street with him before all this started. And yet, they were the only game in town. To be combat-effective, Taggart had to work with the "indigenous population," as he had begun to think of the Resistance. They knew the territory, they had what little intelligence was to be had, and they were the ones with the supplies and the network.

So, as much as it pissed him off, he'd have to work with that piece of shit ganger. Damn. He remembered vividly when they found his cousin's body a year ago, with two bullets to the back of his head. Dimitrius was a troubled teenager, and ran with the wrong crowd, but he'd been a good kid inside. Taggart remembered fondly how the kid had melted the family's hearts, despite being a half-breed. He had charisma, that one. But he had crossed his gang's leader, and despite Taggart's best efforts to get him the hell out of New York, Dimitrius paid with his life for crossing Black's boss.

Taggart had never dealt with Black directly but had seen him and heard about him from his cousin. His name was something else, of course, but Taggart couldn't remember what it was. But Dimitrius had been clear about him—he didn't like "Mr. Black," or any of Black's crew, back in the day. And that '411' comment was something Dimitrius quoted often, usually with a dramatic roll of the eyes and followed by a bunch of shit-talking.

"Very well, soldier," he said to himself out loud. "Suck it up and accomplish the mission. Deal with the world later. Right now, you have orders to follow and job to do: save America. And *then* put a bullet in that little fucker."

Taggart tried to tell himself that was it, that his decision was made, but in truth it would be a daily struggle to keep his mission front and center. But he was a soldier of the U.S. Army, and his personal crap would have to take a back seat to his oath of service. For now.

* * *

Well, Cassy mused, they'd made it back to camp. She explained everything, and now Michael was running around stringing up make-shift booby-traps and alarms around the camp. Cassy had insisted they keep two people on guard at all times through the night, and Michael had agreed. There was no resistance to the idea among the others. It just made sense.

As she stared out into the night, searching, she occasionally saw a bush move or heard a sapling rattle its leaves. Whoever made those noises was otherwise as silent as the dead, however, and they never heard or saw whoever was moving around out there.

Jed stood up. "I'm going out with Michael to look for tracks. I want to know what all we're dealin' with here, and how many of 'em are out there." Without another word, he walked out into the night toward where Michael could be seen rigging some sort of trip alarm with cans on a string. He'd found the cans and other trash all over the woods. Being close to people, it had been misused somewhat as a garbage dump.

Cassy stood and walked to Mary. She was pale and sweaty, still. "How are you doing, sweetie?"

"Well I feel like crap, but Ethan says I'm almost certain to make it without permanent damage. He says I should be 'eighty percent good to go' by tomorrow, or the next day at the latest. I can't wait..."

Cassy chuckled. "Me neither. You really had us worried. Thank the Lord it wasn't a rattler, eh?"

"Yeah. Thank God for small favors. Um, listen, Cassy, can I talk plainly?" asked Mary, and she looked around to make sure no one else was within easy hearing distance.

Cassy nodded and gave a shrug. "Sure, whatever you want. Fire when ready."

"It's kind of awkward. But I guess I should just rip the bandage off with this, so here goes. Do I have anything to worry about with you and Frank? I see how you look at him, and honestly, he looks at you the same way. Of course, only when you both think the other person isn't looking. But I've had a lot of time to just sit and watch you all lately. I'm not accusing you of anything, mind you. It's just that... Well, there's enough dynamite in camp right now, and you know just who I'm talking about."

Cassy froze, and for a second a shiver of adrenaline shot up her spine. But no, Mary wasn't accusing her of anything. And anyway there was nothing to accuse her of in the first place. But did Frank really look at her, too? Another, very different shiver ran through her.

"No, Mary. No. He's a handsome, capable guy for sure,

but he's mighty in love with you and you have a family together. Whatever passing thought I might have, it's just that—a passing thought. Even if Frank tried anything, I'd shoot him down. We got enough problems, like you said, with the Jasmine-Amber bullshit going on. We'll have to deal with that sooner or later, I reckon."

Mary nodded but didn't reply. Apparently exhausted from the effort of sitting up and talking, she leaned back against the tree again and closed her eyes. After a moment, she said, "Thanks, Cassy. I knew you were a good person, with a good head on your shoulders. It's why you and Frank are our unspoken leaders, yeah? Anyway, I need to rest. Have a good night, sweetie."

Cassy smiled. Then she stood and walked back to her log "bench" and sat. She looked around at the campers. These were all her people now. Hers, and Frank's. She just hoped they could keep their bullshit under wraps long enough to get to her farm. Then she passed time running a headcount.

And half-stood, then froze. No no no... Where the hell were Amber and Ethan? Goddammit. She turned to look at Jed; he and Michael were peering at the ground and screwing around with cans on a string still, but that wouldn't last long.

Cursing like a sailor under her breath, Cassy began the rounds of the camp, looking for the missing idiots and feeling sorry for herself that she had to babysit grown adults.

- 12 -

2300 HOURS - ZERO DAY +7

ETHAN AND AMBER sat in one of the lean-tos, the only one that offered any real privacy. He sat as far from her as possible, not yet comfortable with anything more than sitting and talking. But damn, she looked so pretty in the half-light from the fire. Jed didn't know what a good thing he had, and someday soon it would bite him in the ass.

As far as Ethan was concerned it couldn't happen fast enough, but for here and now, until they were safely at Cassy's farm, what he was doing now was as much as he was willing to risk. Amber seemed to understand, thankfully, because she made no effort to move closer. She just smiled at him, and they talked and made jokes at each other's expense. Sometimes rather crude or suggestive jokes, but they were only words, right? He tried to convince himself there was no harm in that.

Ethan continued, "So then Thalis, my DK, or Dark Knight, did a Mirror Blur to boost his DPS and went all 'fists of fury' on the Shaman while Moktar, the Bard, did his Flute of Speed maneuver to dart past their last tank, I think he was a straight Fighter, and we took their Pennant. And so my

Stalwart Blades took yet another castle from those noobs and got, I think, like two thousand Rep!"

Amber smiled and then pretended to yawn. "You already told me this one, oh mighty Thalis. You do know that sounds an awful lot like phallus, right?" She snickered, and Ethan made a big show of having hurt feelings. Amber rolled her eyes and said, "Don't be like that. It's not my fault you got all Freudian with your name."

Ethan chuckled, and couldn't seem to look away from her beautiful eyes. What an amazing woman. "Two thousand Rep is nothing to sneeze at, I swear! We used it to add a level three Enchanting Apparatus to our guild hall."

"Oh? And is it enchanting? Your 'apparatus,' I mean." Amber said it with a straight face, but Ethan saw her eyes crinkle in that alluring way they did whenever she was making a deadpan joke at someone's expense.

"Oh yeah. Level three enchanting, bay-bee! With that, you can work the Apparatus for an hour, four times a day."

Amber choked. "You wish, perv!"

Ethan was about to laugh, too, when the lean-to's flap was thrown open. He looked up in surprise and saw Jed standing in the opening. Jed's eyes were narrowed to slits, and he stood with his hands at his sides balled into fists.

"You sonuvabitch. You think you can just move in on a man's wife? Get up, you bastard. Get up, or I'll kick your ass sittin' down." Jed's voice was flat and emotionless, but his eyes told a different story.

A jolt of fear shot up Ethan's spine. "Wait, Jed, we weren't doing anything, I swear! I was telling her about a castle raid, that's all!"

Another voice, from outside: "What the hell are you doing, Jed?"

It was Michael's voice, and it had the weird, monotone sound Michael got when he was in combat mode. Ethan had a brief hope that Michael would pull Jed away, but that hope was quickly dashed when Michael continued, "And what the fuck is your wife doing in there with Ethan..."

Jed snarled, "Getting his ass curb-stomped, that's what."

Amber stood up and got face to face with Jed. "Stop this! We weren't doing anything wrong, Jed. Why the hell are you such a jealous prick? You think I don't see how you look at Jaz? Who the hell do you think you are?"

"I'm your damn husband, that's who," said Jed, and Ethan thought he looked about ready to hit his wife.

From what Amber said, Jed had never struck her in anger, but he looked ready to do so now. Ethan felt his initial fear turning into anger, and a deep need to get Amber away from Jed. Right now. "Jed, I know you're angry, but she didn't do anything wrong. There's no need for this. Just take a step back, and don't do something you'll regret in ten minutes."

Jed's eyes flicked back to Ethan, and his face was flushed red. "You threatening me, boy? Please say you are."

Michael had been watching the exchange passively, but apparently came to a decision because he reached his hand out and put it on Jed's chest, restraining him and even pushing him back a little. "Jed, it ain't worth it. Not here, not now, and not in front of the whole damn clan. Kids, Jed. They don't need to see this."

That seemed to get through to him. Ethan saw Jed slowly and deliberately unclench his fists as he took a half step back, away from Amber. "This ain't over with, geek. Not by a mile. Stay away from my bitch, y'hear?"

There was a commotion outside the lean-to, and Ethan saw the rest of the adults shuffling into view, all asking the same questions at the same time. What was going on, who did what, the usual questions.

"Well, I was talking to Amber about a castle raid my

guild did in a game I played a lot before the lights went out. Jed here seems to think it was more than that, and wants to defend his wife's and his honor, but Michael points out that the kids don't need to see us fighting. That's all, so far." Ethan's eyes never left Jed's. Let the redneck take a swing, Ethan thought, and he'd find out what Hapkido could do against a brawler... How dare he talk about Amber like that.

Michael frowned and said, "Well, Amber, it doesn't take a Marine scout to notice how you two have been rather cozy lately. If it was Tiffany and Ethan, I'd probably have already taken him out back to work out who's right."

Amber stiffened. "We've done nothing wrong, Michael. There's no law against talking, and that's all it's been. I'm married, after all."

Frank coughed once, and all heads turned to him. "Ethan, no one's going to fight here. Not over this, not yet. But you must understand what it looks like, and how a husband would feel about his wife being overly friendly with another man."

Ethan clenched his jaw and paused a second to consider his words. Then he said, "Frank, Jed, Michael. I can understand how a man might feel about that *if* that man wasn't doing the same thing with a beautiful young woman who isn't his wife, and *if* there was anything going on between his wife and another man. But Jed, you spend more time with Jasmine than Amber does with me because she *respects* you as her husband. Maybe she was just feeling a little left out and needed someone to talk to about things *other* than your relationship issues. Maybe Amber's feelings are hurt, and maybe she's insecure what with you spending so much time with Jaz. Either way, though, I swear to you that she's done nothing to violate your trust."

Jed slowly unclenched his fists, and took a deep breath.

But then Ethan narrowed his eyes and added, "Can you

say the same, Jed?" The prick had probably at least kissed Jaz, he figured, considering how those two made goo goo eyes at each other all the time.

Jed roared and leapt toward Ethan with a snarl on his face.

Before he could get within striking distance, however, Michael grabbed Jed around the waist and by sheer strength dragged him away from Ethan. "Jed! Stop this. Right now!" barked Michael, and the iron tones of military discipline in his voice brought Jed to an abrupt halt.

Cassy stepped between Ethan and Jed, who was a couple yards away with Michael, now. "Stop this at once! You're both acting like you're in goddamn high school. We're a clan, right? So act like it. Ethan's right, Jed—you *do* spend all your time with Jasmine. You and Amber had problems even before the lights went out, right? So maybe just think about this—think about what you want, what you *really* want."

Jed had regained control of himself, Ethan noted. Smug little bastard. Oh sure, he was all high and mighty about marriage vows when his wife *only talked* to another man, but trying to dip his wick in a woman almost half his age was fine? Total bullshit.

* * *

Peter watched the spy's camp through his scope, which he'd unclicked from his rifle to make it easier. Here in these woods, he wouldn't need the scope to shoot a bear, or whatever.

He chuckled when he saw the plump guy with some geek tee shirt almost come to blows with the wiry rough-neck who wore the straw cowboy hat. The soldier—or at least, he moved and acted like a soldier—broke it up before anyone got to swing a punch, but it was clear that whatever the argument was about had the spy's group split down the middle. The cowboy, the soldier, and the older guy who Peter assumed was the group's leader were on one side; the geek, the spy, the old lady, the three wives, and the hot young piece of ass were on the other. Peter's money was on the three men if it came to a fight between them.

As he watched, the cluster of people broke apart, and they all seemed to just go about their business, but Peter noticed that the two "sides" from the argument were keeping mostly separate from each other. He was surprised to see the young woman, whom he had begun to think of as "Hotlips"— a name from an old TV show—was clearly on the geek's side. Surprised, because from what Peter had seen she seemed to be always hovering around Cowboy. Of course, Cowboy's wife had been doing the same thing with Geek. So, whatever was going on there, it had clearly blown up in all their faces.

Good. The rat bastards deserved it. If a man couldn't trust his wife, a little kicking ass was only right. Cowboy's wife shoulda kept her pants on, no matter what her man was doing with Hotlips. Dudes were just wired that way, he decided, and women needed to lighten up about it.

Peter grew bored watching them and sat down, leaning against a tree. He pulled out his pocket-sized journal, a brown leather-wrapped journal he'd picked up from some big-box chain book store. He hadn't used it before the lights went out, but now he kept meticulous notes about everything he saw his prey and her group doing. He'd also taken to keeping a sketch map of his journey with detailed notes, as well, marking down every encounter, every danger, every possible place to resupply his own people when he led them to the Promised Land. If his folk ran low on supplies on the journey, a good leader would know where to raid for more. And he, Peter Ixin, was going to be a *great* leader.

Peter became drowsy as he thought about the perks he'd

enjoy once he took over leadership of his people. Maybe he'd spare Hotlips when they killed the spy and her group because *damn* she had a nice ass and a great rack. Hell, the slut would probably *love* to be under the wing of Peter the Great... Bitches were all the same way, as far as he was concerned. But if he spared her, she was sure as shit gonna *earn* his mercy.

Peter smiled at the thought and then drifted into sleep. His dreams that night were both naughty and nice.

- 13 -

0800 HOURS - ZERO DAY +8

CASSY FOUND IT easier to keep up with the group today than she had yesterday. Her shoulder just didn't hurt like hell anymore, though she still couldn't really use her right arm. Given that the clan seemed split down the middle about the issue with Amber and Ethan, Jed's group might not have waited for Ethan's group to keep up during the day's travels, which would have been dangerous, but Mary was still limping from the snake bite. To Cassy's relief, that meant the clan traveled more or less together. Safer that way, and more chances to heal the rift. At least, she hoped they could heal it.

Mandy hovered nearby as they traveled, always keeping an eye on her daughter. Cassy found it both annoying and comforting. "So, about this Jed thing," Mandy said, "why do you think he's so upset? Everyone in the clan has seen the googly eyes he makes at Jasmine."

Cassy shrugged, then regretted it as the ache in her shoulder briefly flared up. "I don't know, Mom. It boils down to pride, I imagine."

"One of the seven deadly sins, pride is. And maybe it means Jed won't feel better until his pride is healed."

Cassy thought about that for a minute as they walked. "What will it take to fix the problem, do you think? Something other than giving it up to Jesus in prayer, please."

Mandy frowned. "Don't dismiss the power of prayer. I've heard you pray when things get really bad, and it tends to work out for you."

"Maybe. But Mom, what we need right now is something we can do to help. 'God helps those who help themselves,' right?"

"Yes, of course. We can't just sit around and wait for God to fix our problems, but that doesn't mean we can't lean on His blessings when we need them." Mandy paused and shook her head as if clearing out what she thought of as her "preacher mode," since Cassy sometimes had trouble hearing past it. "Anyway, this is an old argument. For the Jed problem, I think Amber needs to stay away from Ethan until Jed decides what he wants to do about Jasmine. He'll have to be the one to make the first real move, or he'll never forgive either Amber or Ethan. Or maybe they should recommit themselves to their own darn spouses."

Cassy ran that around in her mind for a while as they walked. It would definitely be easier if Jed and Amber just fixed things up, but those two had problems even before the lights went out. It just didn't seem very likely both of them would decide to patch things up. That meant someone was likely to "cheat" on the other. And it seemed obvious to Cassy that it mattered a great deal who made the first move.

"Ethan," she said as she sidled up to him. "So, I need to talk to you. Got a minute?"

Ethan smiled at her. "Sure thing, I can push back my lunch meeting with Accounting. What's up?"

"I know Amber means a lot to you. Or she seems to. Am I right? Do you really care for her?"

"Damn, Cassy. I only just met her. But I guess if I'm

honest, I'd say that she's pretty damn amazing. I have no idea why she's with Jed because she's far smarter, but then again intelligence isn't the only thing that draws people together. They must have had something in common at one point."

Cassy said, "From what I've seen, everyone here is Good People—Jed included. He's not the most educated guy, but he's smart. He knows a lot about farming, and from what I've heard he can fix almost any machine—I can't do that despite my fancy degree."

Ethan let out a deep breath, and his shoulders seemed to sag like a tension had left him. "Yeah... I can't do that either. I can change my car's oil, that sort of thing. But what's your point, Cassy?"

"Just this. If he's a good man, and if he's got skills the clan will definitely need to survive, then I need—no, we all need—for you two to get along. We need you both, desperately. It's the whole reason I signed up for this 'clan' thing. No one of us has all the skills we'll need to survive the winter, much less the year after. So, I need to ask you a favor, Ethan."

Ethan walked in silence for a couple of minutes, and Cassy let him stew in his own thoughts for a while. She knew he was a good man too, and smart, but damn if she would get what she wanted by pushing or bullying him...

Finally, Ethan said, "So, what do you need from me? What does the clan need?"

Cassy smiled and put her good hand on his arm, reassuringly. Then she said, "From what I've seen, Amber is pretty into you." She paused as a smile washed over Ethan's face, but it was quickly suppressed. "You two may be a great fit in this dark new world, but for that to happen in a way that's good for everyone, it has to happen on Jed's timeline. That's his wife, and he has his stubborn Dude Pride, just like you do. All I'm asking is that you put the brakes on things until Jed sorts out what he wants and tells Amber himself. Just let him set the pace. Be the better man. Can I count on you?"

Ethan nodded, the movement barely visible, but at least it was a damn agreement. Cassy could only hope he'd follow through. If they were to have the best chance to survive this, the whole clan needed Ethan to go along and get along, at least for now.

"Fine, Cassy. It isn't right, but I see your point. Maybe the best chance for all of us to find our happy in this bullshit world we're in is for us to do this your way."

Cassy saw him force a smile, and she smiled back. Over his shoulder, she saw Mandy nodding in approval. Thank God, because she needed her mom's help to manage the homestead, when they got there. No one could organize a household and manage children like Mandy. Plus, her mom could make her life miserable if she thought Cassy was pushing for a bad solution. Jesus, managing all these people was exhausting.

* * *

Two hours later, Jaz somehow found herself walking near Jed. Yeah, right... So like, okay, she wanted to talk to him. Whatever. She lost her train of thought as she watched Jed, the muscles rippling under his jeans and his shirt as they walked over the uneven ground. The dude was not just hot. He also had a good head on his shoulders, and a good heart. Someone who could take care of her, yeah, but also a guy who could help her get her shit together.

Jed glanced at her and saw her staring at him, and a wide grin flashed across his face. "Well hello there, girl. I thought you weren't talkin' to me anymore, by account of the thing with Ethan."

"I always have time to talk to you," she said with a smile as bright as sunshine. "I just got other ideas about it, that's all."

"Well, as I see it, he's a guy who's all too interested in a married woman. Can't trust a guy like that."

Jaz shrugged. "I have too much interest in a married man, I s'pose." She kept her face carefully cheerful. The last thing she wanted to do was piss off Jed. She had better things in mind, with him.

"It's different, Jaz. Amber's a woman, and I'm a man. That's just how things are in this ol' world."

Jaz watched his face carefully as he spoke, but he seemed calm. So far, so good. "Yeah, I get that. But you know, it seems like that world's dying off, you know? In the old world, you were like, married with kids. But in this new one, we're totally winging it. We're a clan, right? Because we're all stronger together than apart."

She paused a moment, then continued, "So, I'm just thinking out loud here, but aren't you tired of being with Amber? You two were never real good together. You told me. It must be totally exhausting arguing all the time. But me and you don't argue, right? In the old world, me and you would never have been a match, but here and now I think we're pretty damn good for each other."

Jed smirked, and winked at her. "I reckon we are. I surely have thought about ways we could be even *more* good together. I just don't even think of Amber like that anymore. Too much dirty water under that rickety old bridge. But," he said, and paused. "But, that don't make it right for her to be buzzin' around Ethan all day like a bee to a flower."

Jaz nodded once, a sharp move of her head and nothing more. "For sure, Jed, but I can't help feeling like you deserve more than a bad marriage. You really do deserve to be happy, too. And so do I. And Jed? I think about how we could be *more good* together, too. I feel like we didn't cross paths on accident. Maybe Ethan didn't cross Amber's path on accident, either. Just think about if maybe us being a whole clan and stuff is a way out for you, but you still get to keep your daughter. Kaitlyn won't have to miss you, 'cause she's still got you even if you got someone besides her mom to stand by your side."

Jaz practically beamed with joy when Jed smiled at her. He liked the idea! Now if she could just get him to let go of his stupid ego... Jaz thought Amber was pretty cool, and anyway, she probably wouldn't mind being at someone else's side. But, she decided not to press the issue right now. Dudes liked to think some ideas were their own, and Jaz had become pretty damn good at that game growing up. Like, she had to just to survive. But now, for the first time in a long time, Jaz thought that there might be more to her life than just surviving.

"I sure do feel safe with you, Jed. You mind if I just walk with you for a while? We don't have to talk about this stuff. I just want to feel safe for a while."

Jed accidentally-on-purpose bumped into her as they walked, nearly knocking her over, and she stifled a laugh. They walked on in silence, and Jaz was sure he was thinking over the stuff she said. Yeah, it might be turning into a super good day.

* * *

Frank sat down with a groan, legs and back aching. He'd spent the morning's travels watching Cassy buzz around like a bee, talking to one person after another, and whatever she said to them seemed to have worked. Tensions among the group were still high, but noticeably less than they had been.

That Cassy, she was a damn good woman. A good leader too, Frank thought, and soon enough she'd be taking over the lion's share of leading the whole clan after they got to her homestead. The thought made him smile. He had no taste for being in charge, but he'd been the only real choice. Thank God that would change soon.

He looked around as the others got settled in for lunch, except for Michael, who insisted on climbing a tree and standing guard while the others ate; he'd eat while they traveled, after lunch. A good man, that Michael.

Jed sat down next to him with an "oomph" and turned to look at him. "Howdy, Frank. I got the eggs 'n ham MRE, care to trade?"

"You don't even know what I have, Jed," replied Frank with a smile.

"Doesn't much matter. Anything beats green eggs and what they call ham."

Frank exchanged MRE packets with Jed and opened his. "You owe me one," he smirked. Jed only nodded.

"So what did you and Cassy talk about," Frank said, trying to sound nonchalant. "You were chatting for a good while."

"Same ol' thing Jaz talked to me about. And Grandma Mandy, after her. This thing about Amber and Ethan."

Frank noticed Jed's jaw clenching when he mentioned Ethan, but at least he wasn't flexing his fists unconsciously anymore. A good sign. "Well, you know I'm behind you, however it ends up going. You know that, right? But, I gotta say, Cassy makes a lot of sense. She's a good-hearted woman and has a good head on her shoulders. We lucked out clanning up with her, I think. That homestead will be the difference between living and starving, come winter."

Jed looked at his MRE, working through some thought or another. Frank decided that was good and held to a friendly silence, to give Jed room. His reminder about the bigger picture was something Jed already knew, of course, but the stubborn semi-country boy sometimes needed a reminder. Jed had always been hot-tempered, but also a damn good friend.

Finally, Jed replied, "Well, I see that Amber and Ethan aren't glued at the hip today. Feeling better about that. It's a respect thing, I think. I haven't been in love with her in years, but dammit, there's a way to do things and a way not to do 'em."

Frank nodded. "Yeah, that's so. But what are you going to do about Amber and Jaz, now that you're calm? It's a big choice. And I think Cassy's right about your kid being okay as part of a bigger family. I don't think we can afford to build fences between families when it comes to the kids at least. We're all in it together, and as far as I'm concerned, your kid's just part of my family, same as Michael's kids."

Jed frowned but nodded. "Self-reliance was how I was raised, but I'm starting to think that maybe 'group reliance' is more important, now—the whole clan for all, and all for the clan. Not sure where I heard that before, but it rings true."

Frank chuckled. "It was a line from a movie, Three Musketeers. All for one and one for—"

Frank stopped abruptly, and then realized he was hearing a faint roar, growing in volume. "Fuck, planes. Everyone, take cover. To the trees!"

He leapt to his feet and bolted toward a large tree, grabbing his son, Hunter, with one arm as he sped by the sitting child. One glance over his shoulder told him the others were doing the same, everyone scrambling for kids and for trees. Thank God he hadn't built a fire for lunch... And then he was under the canopy of the tree. Crouching down low, he peered around for the source of the engine noise, but even as the roar grew louder, he couldn't yet tell where it was coming from. The noise was bouncing around the woods and rocks too much to tell, yet.

As the noise grew into a full-fledged roar, Frank could finally tell that the plane or planes were coming from the east. Not surprising, he thought. Please, God, don't let them see the clan, he prayed.

The planes came into view through the trees then. Next to him, Michael whispered, "Fighters. Look at the pods on the wings, those are missiles."

"Ours?"

"Negative. It looks like a Flanker, but they don't carry bombs. Gotta be a Fullback. A variant of the Sukhoi, and from what I've read they're damn rare. But that isn't a Russian camo. I don't recognize it—it looks vaguely Iranian, but what does a grunt know about that?"

A lot more than me apparently, thought Frank, once again glad to have Michael's expertise in the clan. If those planes saw his people, they could wipe out the whole clan. Wouldn't that be goddamn ironic, so close to Lancaster they could almost taste it...

* * *

Cassy lay under a tree and bit her lip to keep from crying out. She'd struck her bad shoulder on a large root when she slid into cover. Her daughter, Brianna, and Jaz were under the cover of her tree as well. She frantically looked for her son, Aidan, and only turned again to look at the planes after she spotted him under another tree with Mandy.

The planes were clearly fighters, though she couldn't tell anything more about them except that there were three of them. Studying airplanes was not something she'd had time or desire to do, though at the moment it would have come in handy. She glanced at Frank, who was with Michael, and saw that he was hiding still. So, they were enemy planes. Then she thought how silly it was to have wondered that in the first place—all the planes in the air that she'd seen so far had been those of the invaders. Of course, the EMP must have grounded all the U.S. fighters, just as it had the commercial jet that she'd seen crashed in Philadelphia.

The three fighters were coming directly toward them in a tight wedge formation, one plane in front and the others slightly behind to both sides. As the planes came closer and closer a sense of panic washed over her, and she reached out with her good arm to embrace Brianna to her tightly. At least if they were going to die here, she decided, they would die together...

Just before the planes reached what Cassy imagined was a good distance to drop bombs or whatever, they veered to their right, heading more northerly now. A second later all three planes unleashed several missiles, which streaked away toward the ground. The buzzing noise of their strafing machine gun fire rose over the din of their engines, despite the fact that those engines were now pointed back toward the clan.

Multiple deep booms washed over her, and she felt like it might knock the wind out of her. As her ears rang from the sound, she saw several small mushroom-shaped clouds of black smoke and fire rise up from the ground, maybe only a hundred yards or so from where she lay. What the hell were they shooting at?

In seconds the planes were gone, engines flaring with afterburners as they tore off eastward, no doubt heading back to whatever base they came from. For the moment all was clear.

Michael was the first to stand, she saw, and he waved the "all clear" sign with his hands. The others, Cassy included, began to rise and moved out toward Frank. The flock seeking their shepherd, she briefly thought, then grinned when it struck her how her mom might react to such a sentiment. 'Only Jesus is the Shepherd, Cassy,' she could practically hear her mom's stern-but-level voice correcting her.

As the roar of jet engines faded to faint, rolling echoes, Cassy heard Frank telling everyone to gather around. It was hard to understand him because her ears were ringing so loudly.

When everyone was gathered, Cassy noted their expressions. The kids looked afraid, of course, and so did Jaz. Frank and Jed were calm, or appeared so. Michael was pissed off, as were Mandy and Tiffany, though Amber might have been angry, too. It could be hard to tell with her, sometimes. Ethan, however, looked excited.

Frank spoke up over the hushed questions everyone seemed to be asking, and Cassy realized how silly it was to be whispering after all that noise. He said, "Those bastards were shooting at someone or something, and it wasn't us, thank God. Michael says they wouldn't send so much firepower after refugees, so it has to be either a building or a U.S. military unit."

"Hard target or friendly forces," Michael corrected. He looked so pissed that he could barely contain himself.

Frank nodded, hands up toward Michael, appeasing. "Yes, that. And we all saw how close those missiles were. Maybe a half mile at most. Now, Michael says our duty is to go see if any soldiers survived or, if it was a building, see whether anything can be salvaged. It could be dangerous, though, so we need to be either all in or all out."

Michael spat. "I'm going, one way or the other, Frank. If you all go on, fine—you aren't soldiers, and you aren't Marines, so I understand. I'll have no problems catching up to you later."

Ethan could no longer contain himself. "If it was

soldiers, they may have working vehicles that didn't get destroyed, or radios, or supplies. I'm going with Michael. Plus, if any soldiers survived they may need our help."

Frank nodded as he said, "I agree. I vote we go. Anyone disagree? Speak up if you got another idea."

Everyone looked around at the others, but no one spoke up to disagree. "Fine," Frank said, "then we need to get going right away. We move out in five minutes, so get packed up."

Once again, Cassy was impressed by Frank's level-headed leadership, and his ability to get everyone moving in the same direction quickly. She thanked all the stars in heaven that she'd stumbled into these people.

- 14 -

1215 HOURS - ZERO DAY +8

CASSY STARED IN awe at the scene of destruction. It had only taken them twenty minutes or so to find the site of the air strike, but it was clear at a glance that few could have survived the attack. Two tanks and six of the military Hummers had been moving along an old logging trail, and all were blackened twists of smoking metal, now. There was also an old-style Jeep, which wasn't burning but had numerous huge, jagged holes in it from the strafing jets. Two men inside the open-top vehicle were now mostly chunks of gore. What a jet's guns could do to a human body was beyond terrifying.

"Mandy, take the kids back a bit, please. They don't need to stare at this," said Cassy. Her mother nodded and expertly herded the juveniles away with help from a limping Mary.

Michael put his hands to his mouth and shouted, "Oorah! Any survivors? Sound off like you got a pair." Cassy loved that bark of his—both calm and super loud at the same time. If she had known how to do that, her kids would *never* have disobeyed her growing up...

Cassy heard a voice and jumped in surprise. "Hoo-ah!

"Identify yourself, soldier," shouted a male voice she didn't recognize.

"That's Marine to you, Doggie," replied Michael. "Stand down, we're friendlies. Anyone else survive? Wounded?"

There was a rustle in the scorched brush nearby. Three men in cammo pushed through. Two appeared to be okay, but they were both helping the third soldier, who was bleeding from his leg and had half his hair singed off. "*Semper Fuckyou*, jarhead," said the wounded soldier. He was the one who had talked to Michael, and he wore a huge grin. "So happy you aren't OpFor, even if you are a Marine."

Minutes later, Ethan had done what he could for first aid to the wounded soldier, and the other survivors had gone out and quickly returned. They confirmed there were no others left alive.

The wounded soldier, who said his name was Lt. Harrison, gritted his teeth from both pain and anger. "Those were all the operational vehicles we could muster, goddammit. And I lost near thirty good soldiers today. Fuck all, I can't even write their families."

Michael nodded. "FUBAR, sir. What were your orders, and why were you out here, of all places?"

Harrison let out a loud breath, then said, "We were under orders to head to some dink town near Philly to find a civilian and, if he was still breathing, to help get him back online. Back channel, I was told he was an important asset for the fight against these fucking invading forces. We had a lot of weird computer gear for him in the back of the Jeep."

Ethan looked up in surprise. "Um, sir, can I ask you what was the name of the guy you were going to look for?"

Harrison stared at Ethan for a long while, clearly sizing him up, and then said, "Yeah... Could be... His asset codename was 'Dark Ryder,' and he might just be the only guy still alive and in the region with the knowhow and equipment to help us put up a coordinated counteroffensive."

Cassy looked at Ethan again and gave him a hard stare. What the hell? But Ethan was just some rich conspiracy nut. A gaming freak. Wasn't he?

"I think we need to talk more, Lieutenant," said Ethan, voice shaking.

* * *

For the last hour, Ethan had gathered the gear from the Jeep and inspected it. One was clearly a laptop, but the other items were lost on the rest of the group. Ethan, however, knew what they were, and grinned like a fool. "Only one piece was damaged, and I jury-rigged it with some wiring from the Jeep. No one will mind if it no longer has working turn signals."

Frank shrugged. "Not my Jeep, not my problem. So what is this crap?"

Ethan couldn't keep the joy out of his voice. "This 'crap' is some of Uncle Sam's finest rugged, hardened asynchronous encrypted data transfer and com-link hardware. Some assembly required. But with it, I can get the hell online from anywhere in the world, just about, and get back in touch with some people I was working with after the lights went out. Well… before my bunker was compromised, I mean."

Frank didn't reply, no doubt trying to avoid a conflict. He was a good man, Ethan had long ago decided, but neither Frank nor the rest of the clan could understand what "Dark Ryder" had given up to save their lives. But it had been *his* choice, not theirs, and he held no grudge against them for what had happened because of it.

He was finally able to click the last component into

place, and then connected his laptop and booted it for the first time since leaving his bunker. It whirred and pinged as the desktop came up and it saw new hardware, and it took a minute to find the right drivers from among the files on his loaded-up USB flash drives.

His effort was quickly rewarded. Once the hardware initialized, he loaded the now-familiar "AIR_RDEA" file, and a dialog box popped up along with two dozen new alerts. Ethan noted that they were evenly spaced, so they were automated. It might take a minute for his acknowledgement to be seen. Into the green box he typed,

> *Dark Ryder ack. Temp online. Relocating, connection intermittent.*

It took almost ten minutes for a response.

> *DR: retrieve attached txt file AIR_RDEA 411.txt*

Ethan acknowledged, downloaded the coded text file and ran his decryption routine on it. The data quickly came up, and though Ethan could only decipher parts of it, the picture it painted was bleak. Alaska, British Columbia, Washington and parts of Oregon were eighty percent occupied by North Korea, backed by the Chinese, but they had been halted at the mountain passes in both directions. That wouldn't last long, however, as the defending units were running blind without Ethan's broadcasts and could not respond effectively to an enemy with intact communications.

Additionally, Florida, Georgia, and the Gulf Coast out to New Orleans were similarly occupied by Cuban and Russian forces, but they were spread thin. They'd suffered terrible losses at the hands of a well-armed American populace, though the mortality rate among civilians was already running at twenty percent and climbing. The Gulf State civilians kept coming at the invaders, thinning their ranks, but at a terrible cost.

What Ethan cared about more personally at the moment was the invasion of New York City and beyond. That mostly Arabic and Persian force had occupied the area he had foreseen—a roughly square territory, the borders of which were Baltimore, Cleveland, Buffalo, and Boston. Civilian casualties in the region were upwards of thirty percent, mostly the old and very young, almost all noncombatants. The ISIS-led coalition didn't give a damn about human lives, at least not those among the invading forces.

The enemy unit locations around occupied America, which the file showed by coordinates and coded notations, were thick within those regions, and other than the Koreans in the Pacific Northwest they showed no signs of halting their drives. Everywhere, the invaders were suffering massive losses and delays due to unaffiliated local partisans, but they weren't being stopped in their tracks. For that, America needed a coordinated military response, and the EMP had prevented that so far.

With a sigh, Ethan connected his laptop to the HAM radio on the Jeep and powered it up. With a few deft clicks on the laptop's touchpad, he was broadcasting his coded signal once again, piggybacking on and embedded within a transmission that sounded like nothing more than static. He let the message cycle five times in twenty minutes, then packed up his gear. Hopefully, the new intel would help the remnants of the military and the official partisan groups who could receive it. But now it was past time to get the hell out of Dodge before the enemy noticed and located the transmission.

* * *

1700 HOURS - ZERO DAY +8

Cassy and the clan approached the crest of the hill. Her heart raced, fearing the worst. Out of nervousness, she said, to no one in particular, "I so love Lancaster. It's so old that it has that old-world charm. And the people! Sure, they're mostly conservative types, but they also believe in helping each other, and watching out for each other. My first winter it turned out I didn't have enough firewood, and a neighbor's cousin drove out from Lancaster and spent the day chopping wood for me. Wouldn't take a dime for his work, either, though he did let me feed him a big meal and share a drink or two. Did I mention how *beautiful* the city is?"

They reached the crest of one of the several hills northwest of Lancaster, and looking down, they stared in horror at the scene below. Lancaster, that venerable city, had been a core part at the birth of the Abolitionist movement. For a day, it had been the capital of the U.S. during the Revolutionary War, and it was the city that gave birth to the Pennsylvania Rifle, one of the most important icons of the Frontier Era.

No longer. The Lancaster that lay below them was a burning wreck full of craters and rubbled buildings with no visible moving traffic. The brown haze of death—the noxious gas used by the invaders to destroy agricultural capabilities—lay thick over the city. Looking through the detached scope of a rifle, Cassy saw that nothing moved down there. The ant-like dots of what must be people lay scattered thickly through the streets of the city, but it seemed clear that their suffering was over.

With tears in her eyes, Cassy turned to Michael with a face ablaze in fury. "What can we do?" she asked him, her voice sounding taut and strained even to her own ears. Michael, however, only clenched his jaw and shook his head curtly. No, she realized, there was nothing they could do. Not now.

"Why Lancaster?" said Jed, and his voice broke as he said it. No tears, Cassy saw, but the man was overwrought. "There's nothing in that ol' town worth burning."

Ethan, squatting to Cassy's left, muttered an obscenity and answered, "Yes, there is something there. Or rather, Lancaster's vital for something everyone needs. Food. Lancaster is a major agricultural hub for the whole region. The strategy is evil, and brilliant. By destroying Lancaster, the invaders don't have to divert their forces to haze hundreds of square miles of farms around the town. I doubt a soul remains alive down there, so there's no way to gather, process and ship out any of that food. It'll rot in the trains and on the ground it grew on."

And, Cassy raged inside, millions would starve who might otherwise have at least survived the winter. It was genocide on U.S. soil. The invaders weren't trying to conquer America, or if they were it was secondary. Their goal, the only goal that fit all this evidence, was to utterly destroy America. America the Beautiful. America, land of the free. America, the graveyard. "It's a dark new world in more ways than one," she muttered, and her tears rolled unhindered down her face.

- 15 -

1900 HOURS - ZERO DAY +8

THE SHORT ASIAN man, wearing a crisp North Korean uniform, sat on a simple folding chair in the main room of his tent. Behind him, flaps led to two additional rooms, one for sleeping and the other his office. Flanking him were his two interpreters. Kneeling in a semicircle in front of him, except in front of the entry flap, were six high-ranking members of the ISIS force responsible for The Plan in this part of the U.S. By the People's Honor, he hated these sand-eaters, but they were a necessary evil if the Glorious Leader's plan was to work. And, he mused, they were doing their best to screw it up by killing everyone they could, pissing off the Americans and their idiot allies, and funneling eager recruits right into the waiting hands of the Capitalist counterrevolutionaries, which they gave the romantic label "the Resistance." Pathetic.

He lifted one finger off the arm of his folding chair, and the two Comrade Soldiers at the door opened the flap. Two sand-eaters entered, dragging a bloody mess between them. The Arabs looked as bad as he imagined they smelled, covered in hair and dirt. At least their commanders usually had sense enough to wash themselves before coming into his presence.

The bloody mess, on the other hand, was a pale American with reddish-brown hair wearing that icon of Western decadence, blue jeans, and a tattered black tee shirt. Thankfully he was clean-shaven. Excessive facial hair was a sign of laziness, as far as Ri was concerned.

The soldiers unceremoniously dumped the American on a woven mat in front of Ri and took one step back. Ri stared at the American for several minutes, simply watching and examining him. The American, in turn, couldn't meet his gaze. The Arabs had done a fine job of breaking his spirit. At least they could handle simple torture, even if they screwed everything else up with their foolish reliance on a god.

"Great Leader," he muttered in Korean, "why have you tested me so? My honor is to serve, whatever my own wishes. I thank you for your trust in me for this glorious mission of the People."

The American looked up, but Ri saw no sign of comprehension, any more than he would on the faces of the sand-eaters if he bothered to look at them. Then he said, as his English translator followed almost in unison, "American, why do you resist the will of the People? Do you cling so hard to your MTV and vapid cultural icons that you cannot see the glory of service to the People? Sadly, it seems you do. How are you feeling?"

The American looked up, surprised. "I, uh, I've been better, sir."

Ri chuckled. At least Americans had spirit. Too bad it was so terribly misdirected. "I am Sangjwa Ri or Colonel Ree in your barbaric tongue. Do you wish for water?"

The American nodded, and a petite American woman wearing a dress shuffled to him with a cup, bowed, then backed away. Ri nodded in approval. Americans could be taught to behave, or at least some could. The bloody man drank greedily, then wiped his face with his sleeve. Ri suppressed a grimace, forcing himself to keep his face a mask of stone.

"We have learned you are more than just a misguided rebel. Do you deny this? And what is your name? I forget."

The American kept his eyes averted. "I am Thomas Smith, sir. And I did deny it, for two days. But I wanted these ragheads to quit torturing me, so I said whatever they wanted."

Ri said with apparent nonchalance, "You admitted that you were one of these so-called '20s,' did you not?"

"I've no idea who or what that is, but yes, I did admit it. And would again, if those bastards tortured me again." Thomas shuddered visibly.

Ri suppressed a grin. This one had spirit. No matter, that spirit would soon be crushed when Ri revealed the proof. There was no way the man could be lying, between what he'd said under torture and what his own decoders had found among his possessions.

Ri said, "Pain purifies a man's thoughts and distills them to the essence of Truth. The Great Leader has himself said that the best cure for a disloyal citizen, that is, one who is lazy, is the application of purifying pain. Do you disagree?"

Thomas frowned. "Torture doesn't get at the truth, Ree. Everyone knows that."

One of the guards, on hearing Thomas call him by his simple name, stepped forward with rifle butt raised to strike the American, but Ri held up a hand, and the man stepped back.

"Do not be disrespectful. You lose my respect when you show such poor manners, and that is not good for you. But, you are wrong in what you say. An inexperienced interrogator may get only lies or only the truth he asks for.

But the men who questioned you are well-trained by my people. They distill the salty water of your words into the clear waters of truth. And the truth is, you are one of these Twenties."

It wasn't a question, and the man glanced down before replying, "No, sir, I am just fighting for my home, my people."

With a deft flick of his hand, the colonel produced an SD card. He said nothing, and simply held it up for Thomas to see while he stared at the American to gauge his reaction.

Thomas surprised him by crying out, and his translator was too stunned to catch what he said. Thomas rose to his feet, arm stretched out toward the SD card but was slammed to the ground by a guard's rifle stroke.

Ri allowed himself to grin and chose a good-natured and friendly smile. The arrogance of these Americans. How dare this degenerate Capitalist rise up against him, a Sangjwa of the People's Republic of Korea! But he only allowed his smile to show.

Ri said, "You thought you had hidden this? I see. And so, you thought no harm would be done to your cause if you admitted your role in the Twenties. Interesting. And yet, we broke the ciphers on this in an hour, and already knew what you then admitted, although your questioners did not know until you told them."

Thomas's eyes flowed with tears of anger and fear, and then he slumped. Ri smiled as the man admitted his defeat.

"Yes, misguided Thomas. We have your intelligence. We know where you think our units are. We know where your counterrevolutionary criminal rebels are, and where they are going."

Thomas sobbed. Without looking up, he simply begged, "Please, sir, don't... My country..."

Ri interrupted him, saying, "...is dead. The carcass of

Capitalism will feed the needs of the People, all the People. True authority rests with the People, not your swine leaders, who betray their own people for the fleeting pleasure of a G-5 airplane and personal gain. There is no personal gain! All gain belongs to *all the People*. And now? Now I know the truth of this material. You have betrayed your people by your lack of discipline, foolish American. With this information, all hope is lost, and Capitalism will die a much-deserved death."

Thomas was dragged away, still sobbing, and Ri indulged in a genuine grin this time, before turning to the assembled Arab military leaders attending him. They had much to plan.

- 16 -

1900 HOURS - ZERO DAY +8

CASSY AND THE clan wasted little time staring at the dead city of Lancaster before moving on. Frank and Cassy had decided to take the group north as far as they could before night came fully upon them since it made no sense to stay and mourn a city they were powerless to help. At least trekking on north would get them away from the destruction, and moving, or doing anything productive, would be good for morale. It would also put them that much closer to Cassy's homestead when they started the next day's travel.

Frank had said he wanted to stop at about 2100 hours, and no one had argued. No one had the emotional energy left to argue. They would stop for the night at the east edge of the remote Lancaster Airport, where Cassy knew of a culvert-and-bridge that would be perfect to hide in for the night. Dimmer dusk light would also give them at least a bit of protection against being seen by anyone in the farmhouses scattered about the airport.

Onward they walked, spread out as usual with Michael in the lead, Cassy in the middle with the kids, and the others set up to either flank. There was no rear guard since Mary, still a little sick from snakebite, limped along with Cassy and the kids. It was slow going with the kids and weakened Mary, but no one complained. What choice did they have?

One mile became two, with only about two to go before they would stop for the night. Then an hour to go. Cassy couldn't wait. Her feet hurt and her shoulder, though much improved, still throbbed when she walked. But no infection, she thought. Thank God for Ethan's antibiotics and the first aid she'd received.

Mary interrupted her thoughts. "Cassy, I don't see that brown haze here, but all the plants are that sticky goo. Whole crops, just dead in the fields. Why don't we see the haze?"

That was a damn good question. Cassy didn't have an answer but replied, "Well, if I had to guess, I'd say that it either breaks down into sludge over time, or it converts from gas to liquid at a pretty warm temperature. Say, forty-five degrees. Either would explain the goop that remains when the haze goes away."

Mary looked worried and chewed her lip. Cassy waited as they trudged along. Finally, Mary said, "You told us once that you touched a bit of that goo, and it burned your skin until you got it off. If the haze turns to sludge instead of breaking down, how long will it stay there? And what happens when it rains—will it wash into the water supply?"

Cassy raised her eyebrows at Mary, surprised. "Wow, Mary. My mind has been on keeping us alive until we get home, but those are sharp questions. And the answers will be important before long. You should bring it up when we stop."

Mary beamed with pride at the compliment, a broad smile on her face. Cassy recognized it as the pride people feel when someone in authority pays attention. When did she become someone in authority?

After thinking for a moment, Cassy continued, "In fact, I

think you should tell your ideas to Ethan. He's the geek among us, and I know he isn't the most popular guy right now, but he's important to our survival—and maybe to the survival of America, for all we know, with all that secret squirrel stuff. If any of us can figure out that brown haze and sludge work, he can. We should be stopping in an hour, maybe talk to him then."

Mary nodded and kept walking as they refocused on the kids in their care.

* * *

Jaz stood inside the culvert with the rest of the clan, effectively hidden underneath the small, paved bridge across the drainage channel. Ethan said it was about 9:00 p.m. It was good that Cassy knew the area so well, or they would have missed the small hiding place completely. The culvert provided a good place to camp for the night, so long as it didn't rain. Frank even authorized a very small fire, though without much around that would burn well, the best they could manage was to keep a bed of coals going. But it was way better than nothing, Jaz mused, and the warmth raised her spirits a bit. Smiling, she drank the last of her water. Cassy said she was, like, totally sure they'd reach her farm tomorrow and Michael said there were streams and stuff between them and the farm if they had to stay outside another night. But Jaz knew if she was really thirsty, Jed would share his water with her. He was always doing little stuff like that for her, and it was totally cute. And awesome. All he wanted back was a smile, at least so far, and he treated her with respect. She never met someone like that on the streets. It was confusing sometimes, but she loved the feeling it gave her.

As the others sat around the small fire—still split into two sides, which was emo-sad—Jaz saw Jed get up and walk to the entrance of the tunnel thing they were in. He stood there leaning on the wall with one hand, the other hand in a pocket. He looked absolutely yummy there, a silhouette in the dim light of the rising moon. My cowboy and my gentleman, she mused, and her pulse rose a bit as she watched him.

After a few minutes, when no one went to Jed and the rest of the clan was deep in their conversations, Jaz quietly stood, and walked over to him. She stood a couple feet away. "Keeping up appearances for the Joneses," Jed had called it when he asked her to be more discreet. She guessed that the Joneses must mean Amber and Ethan, but she hadn't asked.

For several minutes, she simply stood there near him and was totally just enjoying his silent presence. It gave her a warm, fuzzy feeling in her tummy to be near the man, and her insides felt like they were bubbling like a shook up can of Coke, all jittery on the inside and calm on the outside. She smiled as she thought about releasing the pressure inside her when she finally slept with Jed. Would she explode like when you open a shook up can, or would the pressure bleed off a little at the time until she was empty inside, completely sated? She could barely stand the wait to find out.

Her delicious thoughts were interrupted when Jed turned to her and smiled. Every day that went by, that smile made her tummy feel funnier and funnier, like totally jumbled up. She could hardly think straight when he did that.

"I've been thinking about us, Jaz. About you and me."

Jaz barely managed to hold in her delight, but she kept her cool and only said, "Yeah? And what have you been thinking, mister? I hope it's nothing appropriate in front of kids." Though she kept her face straight, she thought her eyes must be glowing from her lighting up so much at the thought.

He chuckled, a deep and warm sound that always made her feel like the world was okay, that everything would be like totally fine in the end. "Sort of. You see, I think it's time I got to fish or cut bait. Time to get off the fence and jump in with both feet."

"Definitely go fish, Jed. Jump right in, already!" This time, she couldn't contain her grin and felt foolish, but she just didn't care. Let the world see her act like a fool! It would be fine, so long as she had Jed with her.

"Yeah, well. You see, we're gonna reach Cassy's farm tomorrow, more 'n likely, and I think maybe we ought to have things sorted out before we get there. I think maybe it'd be good if the farm was a fresh start for everyone, not just from the war, but from each other, too. So, in the morning, I'll talk to my wife and tell her what's what, how I feel, how I think she feels, all of it. We're going to figure out what we want to do, and then just move on from there. When the clan gets home tomorrow, I reckon we all ought to stay with who we want, not who we brought, and just call it good."

Jaz thought her heart was going to burst through her throat, or she was going to pass out. It was hammering so hard... "Don't tease a girl, Jed. That's not nice. Tell me you mean it," she said, and her voice cracked on the last part as she said it.

"No fooling. If you'll have me, I want you to be with me. Let Amber have Ethan if she wants him. We haven't been in love in years anyway. I just let my fool pride get in my way. Frank says I do that a lot, and I guess he's right. So now it's time for all of us to just be honest and say it like it is. Let the chips fall, and get on with our life. A brighter, happier life, I hope. It will be if you say yes. Jaz, after I talk to Amber, say you'll be my girl. Tell me you want that, and I'll swallow my pride. You're worth it. The way I get to feeling, when I'm with you, is worth it."

Jaz bounced on her toes a couple times and barely restrained herself from wrapping her arms around Jed right then and there, in front of God and everyone. She stopped, took some deep breaths. It totally didn't help, she was still wound up so tight. "Yes, Jed. Yes!" she squeaked.

Jed looked down at Jaz, his eyes gazing into hers, and she felt like she was swimming in Jell-O. All slow, and totally like some dream. He smiled, and she knew it then. She felt it in her bones. Jed was her man, the one she'd been waiting for, and after tomorrow, nothing in her life would ever be the same again. Real life was about to start for her, not just getting by. Not just like, surviving. She was going to be the best wife a man ever had, she was totally sure of it.

Jaz had a hard time getting to sleep that night.

- 17 -

0400 HOURS - ZERO DAY +9

CAPTAIN TAGGART WAS eating a stack of fast-food burgers while watching TV, but when his home got invaded, he got quickly drawn into a firefight. He called on the other soldiers in his unit to direct fire on the machine gun nest outside his living room, trying to pin down the enemy, but his men were going down all around him until he heroically charged the enemy and destroyed their sniper nest with a grenade. As he stood around celebrating, however, the noise of gunfire didn't go away. He looked around, confused, as the sounds grew louder. His surviving men didn't seem to notice. And then Pvt. Eagan grabbed and shook him, shouting that the enemy was all around, which was odd because Eagan hadn't even been there when he started eating burgers.

It dawned on him that he must be dreaming, and then like a light switch, his view jolted from his living room into the room he shared with Eagan, and the sounds of gunfire growing louder as Eagan shook him. He tried to focus on what the real Eagan was saying.

"Captain! Get the fuck up, sir! We're under attack,"

screamed Eagan.

Taggart leapt from his makeshift bed and snatched his M4, which he always left leaning against the wall next to his bed. "SitRep, Private," he shouted back as his head cleared.

"Multiple armed civilians, unknown number, bearing mil-grade weapons, approaching from the north. They're shooting anything that moves, sir, and they're coming this way like they knew we were here."

"Where's Mr. Black, and what are we doing about it?"

"Sir, he's rallying his men and organizing points of defense, but they're being forced back all over the place! If we don't get out of here soon, we'll have nowhere to go." Eagan took a deep breath and all but yelled, "*Sir, we got to go right now!*" He was almost drowned out by the din of the battle outside.

"Get anyone else still here and rally them in the family room. One mike, upstairs. Move it!"

Eagan sprinted out the door, rifle in hand, and Taggart began to stuff his rucksack with his gear and the few MREs he'd set aside. He had only a minute to get packed himself and get Eagan's gear squared away as well. He finished the job haphazardly, hefted both packs in his left hand and ran out the door holding his rifle in his right, racing toward the family room.

When Taggart entered, he found Eagan there with three others, all Militia men, and spared a moment to thank God that they all had their backpacks with them. The "civilian Militia" guys were always ready to move out in only a few minutes, and though he didn't know their battle readiness, at least they seemed well-trained.

Eagan said, "Sir, update. Black and his guerrillas have been forced back to a point south of our position and are trying to disengage. Militia says he has a rally point under a bridge one klick south. We are behind what passes for enemy lines, now. The OpFor are irregulars from a gang leader north—"

Taggart interrupted him. "Yes, north of us. A traitor and a slaver. But how the fuck did they get intel on our safe houses?"

"Do they have that, you think, sir?"

One of the Militia said with a tone full of contempt, "Of course, soldier. Else how would we be getting pushed back everywhere? That damn Spyder has to be getting intel from somewhere."

Taggart nodded and said, "But irrelevant how. We need exfiltration ASAP before we get overrun." He pointed at the Militia man who'd spoken up. "Is there a subway or something nearby that can get us closer to the rally point?"

The man grinned, his perfectly white teeth a stark contrast to his ebony features. "Yes, sir, we got a hidden door three blocks east, in unclaimed turf. The tunnel runs southwest. It's old, not on the maps. I'm Alex, by the way."

Taggart racked his M4, loading a round into the chamber. "Very good, Alex. We'll avoid contact with the enemy if possible and follow your lead. Move out, mister."

They rushed down the stairs in pairs with Taggart in the middle and Eagan in front with Alex, but before they had all descended Eagan and Alex stopped and turned to run back upstairs.

Eagan shouted, "Sir, out the window! There's a half a dozen people approaching, and they ain't ours."

"Back to the family room! Hustle," shouted Taggart, and turned to run back up the flight of stairs.

When Taggart reached the top, he turned and waved Alex and Eagan to move faster. Just as Alex reached the top of the stairs, there was the loud *BANG* of a shotgun followed by the thump of a foot on the front door, and it flew open. Taggart fired off two rounds through the doorway, and when a loud baritone scream rose from the other side, his blood sang with the joy of battle. Goddamn morons, he thought with joy. They were learning the first lesson of breaching tactics—doorways are kill zones.

Even as his target screamed, Taggart was turning to sprint to the family room. "Window! Go, go, go!"

Alex sprinted past the other two Militia and with arms raised in front of his face he leapt through the window. Glass shattered and seemed almost to explode as he went through. Taggart saw him fall a mere five or six feet to the roof of the carport, followed by Eagan.

Taggart crouched by the window and turned to motion the other two Militia through; both were guarding their rear in case more of the enemy came up the stairs.

At Taggart's command, they turned away from the family room doorway toward the window. A light in the corner of his eye caught his attention. He glanced at the source, and saw, through the windows facing the street, the savage glow of an RPG lighting up the street outside. In the split second of light, he saw that the street outside swarmed with AK-armed men firing in all directions, some shooting kneeling civilians.

And then the RPG came screaming through the bay window. He didn't have time to react before it exploded against the opposite wall, where the two Militia were seemingly moving in slow motion. The Militia men were engulfed in a terrible ball of fire and shattered wall; the flames and concussion struck Taggart like the Hammer of God, and he was flung backwards through the window, flames and debris chasing him out.

The heat seared his face, and the shrapnel pierced him in a dozen places. He flew past Eagan and Alex, beyond the span of the carport, fell ten feet and landed in a heap, skidding to a halt on his back. The light of the fire faded, and the blackness that replaced it was more than just the return of night. He felt hands under his arms, pulling him up, but then the abyss swallowed him, and Taggart's vision faded as he lost consciousness.

* * *

0900 HOURS - ZERO DAY +9

Colonel Ree sat in the elegant chair in his "office," one of three chambers in the large tent. Across the hand-carved desk were neat stacks of paper, folders, and photographs, along with his personal laptop. On the wall opposite the chair hung his "war map," a laminated wall map of New York City. Various notes and marks were scribbled on it. He could have used his computer for that, but he felt it was easier to see the total picture in the vast sweep of a good old-fashioned map.

"Major Mohamed," he said, and tuned out the drone of his translator. "Thank you for coming. I wish to congratulate you on the capture of the American agent of the so-called '20s.' The information my men gleaned from him was most valuable."

The major frowned. Ree was disgusted at the sand-eaters' lack of discipline. Ree kept his face carefully neutral. "Major, do you have a concern? I have congratulated you, yet you seem dissatisfied."

The major paused, then replied, "Colonel, it appears the intelligence you obtained was good. We have been able to strike at several Resistance nests. And yet, many of them were not where the intelligence said they should be, or they were forewarned somehow. And this American gangster, "Spyder," you have given him weapons and set him loose on his rival to the south. Not only did he find what appeared to be a Resistance headquarters and slew many of them, but he also captured many months of supplies. Worse, the leader of that Resistance cell fled with most of the American soldiers he was hiding, and dozens of his brothers in the Resistance. How did they know death was coming for them, and where are they now?"

Ree did not frown. He would never frown in front of this barbaric sand-eater, but Ree was infuriated by the insolence of the man. "If they were forewarned, it was because your men lack discipline. What was it the Americans said during World War II? 'Loose lips sink ships,' " he recited in the original barbaric English tongue. "And yet, with my leadership we moved quickly and decisively. We have captured dozens of American rebels. We killed a dozen American soldiers. We have destroyed a Resistance headquarters, gained hundreds of new workers who will now bask in the glory of Service to the People, and will be taught the power and majesty of the Great Leader before they die. And you question this?"

"I am certain it is as you say. But more escaped than were captured or killed, and they knew we were coming. Your tool, Spyder, now has a hundred men with military rifles and ammunition and, worse, we estimate that he seized months of supplies. What does your tool need from you now? Perhaps he warned his foe so that the Resistance would continue to be a thorn in your glorious side. With those fighters on the loose, perhaps he thinks you will not be strong enough to take back the weapons you gave him. Will he turn over to the People the supplies he seized? You know that he calls himself a king. Now he can be one in truth."

"Indeed. But that would be folly. It occurs to me that perhaps we should relieve him of the weapons and supplies that rightfully belong to their conquerors as spoils of war, and to the People. But Major, you overestimate the danger posed by these rebels. The head has been cut off the snake, and though it may squirm for a while, it is no longer dangerous, and death comes for it soon. Already I have ordered your men to move in on dozens of their supply caches, which we learned of through the weak-minded agent of the 20s. In war, a single mistake can spell disaster as they will soon learn. By the end of this glorious day, the Resistance will be barely a memory of the past."

The major pinched his nose and then, possibly remembering who he was speaking to, he straightened up again. "And of course, Colonel, we will remove Spyder's head as well, yes? That is another snake that needs killing."

Ree waved his hand at the major dismissively. "Of course, of course. Now go practice cutting heads off of infidels, or whatever you do when you aren't being useful. I have planning to do."

Major Mohamed stiffened, jaw clenched and eyes narrowed, but then regained his composure. He saluted, spun crisply, and walked out of the tent.

Colonel Ree allowed himself to smile. Of course the major would suffer insult without retribution. Not only was he weak, like all the sand-eaters, but without Korea's and China's military aid, and the American imperialistic arms manufacturers who sold to whoever had money, they would still be killing each other with swords in the desert, not carving up the rich carcass of America with their "allies." The Glorious Leader was wise indeed to have made the so-called "Axis of Evil" a reality. Ree silently thanked the former President who gave the Leader that idea with his silly rhetoric, and the later President who made it so easy for all this to happen.

"When the evil of Capitalism seeks to appease the righteous wrath of the noble People, they only compound the interest they must pay in blood when their time of reckoning arrives. So says our Great Leader, praise his wisdom and courage."

Ree then removed a bottle of Bourbon from his desk—one of several guilty pleasures—and poured a glass to celebrate the demise of the Resistance, and the glory he would receive as the instrument of their doom. Ree allowed himself to smile again. As always, it was no reflex, but the conscious decision of a disciplined mind. Still, a grin seemed appropriate, just now. He allowed his grin to broaden.

"I shouldn't doubt our Great Leader will reward my ingenuity, but what to humbly suggest for that reward? Hmm. I hear Virginia is beautiful and lush..."

- 18 -

0900 HOURS - ZERO DAY +9

CASSY AND THE clan continued north of the airport for several hours after starting out just before dawn. Then, coming to the woody banks of Hammer Creek, they paused to decide how to proceed.

Cassy, with a faraway look in her eyes, said aloud, "I love this area. My husband and I used to come here often to fish, either at Speedwell Forge Lake or at Conestoga River, back past the airport. They drained the lake a couple years ago, but they refilled and restocked it with fish a few months ago. Fishing used to be good there. My husband always went for the walleyes, and I went after the smallmouth bass. Usually, we had bass for dinner…"

Frank stood next to her, unusually quiet. Finally, he replied, "You've never spoken of your husband before."

"Nor will I again," replied Cassy with her jaw clenched.

Frank diplomatically changed the subject. "I doubt those fish are safe to eat now, and the water's probably bad, too. Damn invaders. Mary was right last night—that goo *must* have gotten into the water. And it's probably poisoning the water table as well unless it breaks down on its own."

Cassy rubbed her eyes with the thumb and index finger of her left hand. Goddamn invaders and all that crap they sprayed. They all ought to rot in hell. The thought cheered her somewhat, and she said, "We'll need water eventually, but I think we can make it until we get to my farm even if we run out of water. Ethan can try to figure out the sludge when we get there. It's not too far now. So, what next, fearless leader?"

Cassy had said that last word with a forced smile. Frank was a good man, and he didn't deserve to get burdened by her damn problems on top of all the other weight riding on his broad shoulders. Such nice shoulders, but of course a catch like Frank already had a woman. Mary was a great person, and they seemed happy together, so she buried the wistful thought.

"Now we have to get across the creek," prodded Frank. "It's not too deep this time of year, thankfully, but it's still either wade across or find a bridge. I don't think we should swim in it. Who knows what got sprayed upriver."

"There's a small bridge just north of us at Brunnerville Road. There's nothing but light farming on the other side, so there's lots of cover and not a lot of people. Then it's a straight shot to my place, but we'll go around and come in from the far side, hidden, so we don't get seen, and we have cover if someone's squatting."

Cassy heard Michael grunt in approval from somewhere behind them, and felt unreasonably proud of that. She cheerfully recognized it as the same pride Mary had felt at Cassy's praise yesterday. If the Leatherneck approved of her idea, it must be sound, although of course the devil would be in the details. She was sure Michael could handle those, though, and she looked forward to learning more from him. The man was quiet, but he sure knew his stuff.

A half hour later they were looking at the bridge from the

cover of trees and scattered shrubs. Michael, in front, crouched motionless facing the bridge. The clan huddled a dozen paces behind him, waiting patiently for his decision. Some fifteen minutes later, an eternity to Cassy, he raised his hand and motioned the clan to gather. Cassy shuffled forward, staying as low as possible, as did the others.

When they were all crouched by Michael, he said in a low voice, "It looks clear. We've got about a hundred yards of open ground before the next cover." He pointed to a copse of trees north and just east, on the far side of the bridge. "I haven't seen movement anywhere, which is good, but those trees make an awesome ambush spot. I imagine the enemy is still thin on the ground here and haven't solidified their positions. We have to get to those trees, regroup, and then we should be clear. But getting there will be risky."

Cassy wanted to ask why he never whispered but always spoke in a low voice instead, but this wasn't the time. Like the others, she nodded her understanding. Without being told, everyone took up their familiar positions. The clan was getting the hang of this, she thought with pride.

She heard the countdown, and on "three" they moved out across the bridge in a single rush, moving fast in a low crouch. But rather than continue down the road as she'd expected, Michael led them to the right, east away from the road by about twenty yards before veering north once more toward the trees, and the clan followed. She had the sudden thought that if there were an ambush ahead, it would likely have the road targeted for the kill zone, and a jolt of adrenaline shot up her spine. Thank God she'd met the clan. No way in hell she'd have made it home on her own, despite all her training and preparation.

They were fifty yards from the trees when Cassy heard the *bang* of a rifle report. Michael dropped onto his stomach shouting, "Down, down!" and the clan followed suit. A half second later the copse of trees lit up with flashes, and the air became thick with the hum of bullets whizzing overhead. Little tufts of dirt flew up all around them as the enemy laid down heavy fire.

To the left, along the road, Cassy heard a series of explosions. She looked over and saw that they were going off in a chain, all along the road—it had been mined. Why the fuck did they ignite them, or whatever, when the clan wasn't on the road? Well, fuck her shoulder, it was time to try out her fucking rock and roll death rifle. She swung her M4, which so far had been mere decoration, forward and planted it firmly into her wounded shoulder. Part of her wondered why it didn't hurt. Time to fire. She aimed for one of the flashes in the woods and fired a single round. She was rewarded with a scream from the tree line, but then by God, she felt her damn shoulder. Ice picks were being jammed into the socket. But Cassy gritted her teeth and kept taking single, aimed shots whenever she could get her head up before being pinned down again.

Michael, in the lead still, was the main target. He seemed to be hiding behind a tiny rock, lying as flat as he could. To his left, Cassy saw Jed crawl on his belly like a snake toward the trees. When he was twenty feet away from her, Cassy saw Michael throw something toward him, and he scooped it with his arm and drew it to himself. Then Michael laid down heavy fire of his own, but Cassy saw that he wasn't aiming. This must be suppressive fire, she thought, and fired off the rest of her magazine toward the enemy. The rest of the clan followed suit. The enemy fire dwindled to nothing for a precious few seconds.

Cassy reloaded as fast as she could with her throbbing shoulder, and as the clan paused to reload the ambushers resumed firing. Cassy felt the wind of a bullet passing inches from her head and went completely prone. As she flopped down flat, her shoulder struck a small rock and a burst of pain mushroomed from her wound. She saw stars and realized she was close to blacking out, so she squeezed her eyes shut and focused on breathing, trying to ignore the deadly whir of enemy bullets all around her.

* * *

Peter watched the battle through his scope as the spy and her new friends struggled against whoever was in those trees. She deserved whatever she got, dammit, but he sensed they were getting closer to wherever they were headed—they hadn't even stopped to refill their water at the creek. But no, God would never let the bitch die now, not when he was so close to learning the location of their base, so close to becoming the savior and leader of all his own people. And yet from his position he couldn't even see the ambushers, much less do anything to help the spy survive the trap she was in. She and her cronies were on their own.

To their left, Peter saw the one he called "Cowboy" crawling ahead toward the ambushers. The soldier guy threw something small toward Cowboy, who scooped it up under a hail of enemy fire. To their right, "Geek" was pinned down, as was "Soldier." Things looked grim for the spy and her people. Peter grinned and cursed at the same time.

There was a motion in the trees, and Peter saw something small fly through the air toward Soldier, but it landed well short. It exploded, sending dirt and shrapnel all around—a grenade, poorly thrown.

In the few seconds of dust and smoke cover, Cowboy leapt to his feet and dashed ahead, then flopped down again onto his belly. He was now within the ambusher's grenade range, if they'd seen him. Reckless. On the other hand, now Cowboy was within grenade range too, if he had one. But of course a grenade *must* be what Soldier had thrown to him. Nothing else would make sense of what they were doing. Where the fuck did they get a grenade?

As if on cue, everyone in the spy's group opened fire at once, save for Cowboy and Geek. The ambushers' fire petered out to nothing for a moment, and in that time, Soldier threw something small toward Geek, who scooped it up. Where the hell was Soldier coming up with them? They couldn't possibly have too many more.

They all stopped fire at once, and Peter saw they were reloading. The ambushers once again fired on the group, and the exchange of shots resumed. The next minute or two would determine everything, and Peter gulped. God, let that bitch survive—she still had a purpose to serve. Fuck the rest of 'em.

- 19 -

0930 HOURS - ZERO DAY +9

ETHAN LAY AS flat as he could after grabbing the grenade Michael had thrown him, ignoring the warm wetness that flowed between his legs. He'd pissed himself when he exposed himself long enough to grab the grenade. Thank God he'd thought to give a couple of those to Michael from his bunker's secret stash of mil-grade gear. It had been a tough choice due to weight issues, but Ethan figured Michael had the training to make it worth the added bulk. Now the extra weight might pay for itself and then some.

The enemy didn't seem to know he was there, nor Jed on the other side of the clan's position—all the enemy fire was toward Michael and the rest. Ethan thanked his lucky stars he had thought to ditch his bulky backpack at the first sign of enemy contact, and that Michael had the good sense to stay off the road. Those mines would have ended things real quick if they'd been in that kill zone when they went off. Maybe them setting off the mines meant they had set them off in a panic, and if so, that meant they weren't facing crack troops. Probably, that was the only reason the clan still lived.

Ethan considered their tactical position, as best he knew

how. Michael was their only real soldier with actual combat experience, but he was pinned down tight. Even so, he'd had the steel to take fire while signaling Ethan and Jed what he had planned, and then again every time he sent a grenade to one of them. Goddamn, Michael had a set of brass balls, endangering himself and his family like that to set up this flanking maneuver. Of course, the entire clan was pinned down, so likely this was their only hope to survive. Michael sure was cool under pressure... Best not to screw this up, yeah. They wouldn't get a second chance.

His heart raced, and the sound of its beating almost drowned out the sounds of battle, but he forced himself to stay perfectly still, focused only on Michael. He'd soon give the signal that would spell victory or death for the clan. Do or die time. Ethan noticed the sounds of shooting taking on an almost rhythmic pattern—fire, receive enemy fire, fire again —a deadly dance that had a sort of raw beauty to it. Nothing at all like the ebb and flow of battle during his video game binges. There was no respawn point here. Beautiful and terrible, this waltz of death was mesmerizing.

He heard the single shrill cry of a whistle, Michael's signal for the clan to reload. There was a pause in their fire as everyone in the center shoved fresh magazines into their M4s, depleting the stock Ethan had distributed to them at his bunker. A second's pause, and then two short blasts of the whistle—the signal to lay it on. The clan risked exposing themselves enough to pour fire into the enemy's position, and the return fire ceased. While they laid it on thick, Ethan bolted to his feet and raced toward the tree line; opposite him, Jed was doing the same. They reached the trees at about the same time, just as the clan ran out of ammo and began to reload.

When the enemy began firing again, Ethan heard the *thump, thump* of bullets striking the thick tree he hid behind. He'd been spotted. Fuck and damn. He paused to count slowly to five, to calm himself for what must come next.

One. Bullets tore chunks of wood off the tree.

Two. A cry of pain came from somewhere behind him; someone in the clan must have been hit.

Three. Cries of alarm from the enemy's position.

Four. A huge *boom* nearby, and the sound of something like rain pattering off the trees all around him.

Five! Ethan leapt to the side, grenade ready, and lobbed it toward the enemy.

As the grenade left his hand, Ethan saw the scene unfolding at the emplacement. The enemy had a sandbagged position with entrenchments, facing the road. It was in shambles, with bleeding bodies draped over the emplacement walls, enemy soldiers caught in the blast of Jed's grenade. It looked to have landed just outside the protective wall of sandbags.

But Jed hadn't dropped—he now stood at the edge of the emplacement, pouring rifle fire into it. Jed's face was red with rage, and Ethan saw his mouth open as though screaming, but all Ethan heard was his own heart beating.

Ethan's grenade continued its deadly arc, now falling toward the emplacement. Two red flowers bloomed over Jed's belly as the enemy soldiers returned fire on him, but he didn't stop shooting into their position. Ethan opened his mouth to scream, to warn Jed of the grenade, but no sound came out. Or if it did, Ethan couldn't hear himself screaming. Either was possible. And then his grenade landed dead center in the enemy's emplacement even as Jed's rifle bursts lit up his twisted, enraged face. It was surreal, and Ethan knew what would happen next.

* * *

There had been no more gunfire after the second grenade went off, out there in the woods. Frank waited for an eternity, it seemed, before standing, and the rest of the clan followed his lead as he walked toward the enemy emplacement with his rifle at the ready. "Cassy, stay here with the kids, and keep them low until we see what's up."

Cassy turned toward the children, who still looked like they were ready to soil themselves. Frank continued toward the trees. Time enough to calm the kids when he was sure they were safe.

When he got to the copse of trees, the scene was like something out of a movie. The ambushers wore the uniforms of the invaders, as he'd expected, and there must have been over a dozen of them. They were sprawled out on the ground and in a sandbagged pit, covered in dirt and blood. Frank shuddered at what a grenade could do to a human and decided the movies didn't do it justice.

To the left he caught sight of Ethan, kneeling with his back to Frank, vomiting into the pit. "Ethan, you injured?" Frank asked, and even to his own ears his voice sounded flat and lifeless. Ethan did not reply, but instead turned to look back at him, tears streaming down his face. Frank didn't see any blood on him, though.

"Where's Jed?" asked Amber as she caught up to Frank.

Ethan still said nothing. He just turned back around. Frank walked the several paces to stand beside Ethan and realized why the man was crying. Jed lay on the ground before him, his head on Ethan's lap, his eyes open and lifeless. Frank saw the two bullet wounds in Jed's gut, and then realized there was also a fist-sized chunk missing from the left side of Jed's neck. No blood pumped from the terrible wound.

Frank saw Jaz sprint towards them and skid to a halt on her knees, next to Jed. She draped herself over the body, sobbing. Amber, too, had begun to cry, her face white as if in shock. She slowly kneeled next to Jed and Ethan, placing one shaking hand on Jed's forehead.

"What happened, Ethan," demanded Frank through clenched teeth. Every part of him wanted to kill someone, anyone, to let out the rage he felt as he looked down at his friend's corpse. But there was no justice in this life; he reminded himself. Over and over in his head he told himself he had responsibilities, now more than ever. His right-hand man was dead. When Michael had shown everyone how to throw a grenade, the drill was to throw and drop. *Why had Jed gone cowboy instead? Why didn't he drop?*

Frank blinked himself out of that pointless train of thought. But really, what would he do without Jed? Jed was always the outgoing one, the negotiator, reining in Frank's tendency to go 'quiet and scary' under stress, as Jed put it. Or, used to put it. Sonsofbitches took more than his friend, they took part of *him,* too. Frank wished he could deal with this better, maybe weep and rail at the gods and then move on, but like everything else in this life, he had to stay strong now and cry later, on his own time.

Ethan wiped his face with his sleeve, and slowly stood with knees shaking. "My grenade got a couple of them, but then they had me pinned," Ethan said unsteadily. "Jed just... He charged them, and even after he was shot he didn't slow down. He threw his grenade into the pit with them and poured on the gunfire until it went off. He sacrificed himself to save... to save *all of us.*"

Ethan's story made a kind of sense, but it didn't sound like Jed, who could be wild and hot-headed but was rarely reckless. Frank stared at Ethan, gauging the man. Ethan had turned away, back toward Jed's body and the two women crying over it.

Something about Ethan's reaction just didn't sit right.

Now, Frank was no master psychologist, but he damn sure knew how to read people. If that sonofabitch was lying, Frank decided, he'd rip off Ethan's junk and choke him to death with it. But why would he lie? *Why didn't Jed throw and drop?*

"Now's not the time for this," said Michael in a low tone.

Frank thought something about Michael's voice sounded wrong and looked over at him, but couldn't read his expression. Michael was bleeding down the outside of his left leg, but it didn't look bad.

"You're hit, Mike." Frank lacked the energy to dig into whatever was on Michael's mind.

"A scratch. I'll be fine. Worry about Amber. No, worry about his daughter—Kaitlyn's only seven and she just lost her daddy."

Frank thought about having to tell Jed's daughter that he was dead, and a shudder ran down his spine. Thank God Amber would take care of that task. "Michael, do me a favor and strip all the gear you think we can use, and bring it out to the clan. Then we'll take care of your leg, and burying Jed. We need to reload and be ready before we can do anything else, though, so let's get to it."

Michael nodded and jumped into the pit of dead soldiers to rummage through their packs and pockets. Frank had to turn away.

He saw Amber then, slumped and kneeling, and spoke. "Amber, I'm sorry for... No, that doesn't cut it. My heart's with you, Amber. That's all I can spare right now."

Jed's wife looked up at Frank, tears streaming. "What am I going to do, Frank? How will I care for Kaitlyn without her daddy?"

Frank saw fear on her face, and his heart truly went out to her. This was no time for that discussion, so he said simply, "You're in the clan. Kaitlyn's in the clan. We take care of our own. That's the way it's got to be now until things get back to normal. If they ever do. Got it? We take care of our own, for better and for worse. *We are a clan.*" The final words came out like Bible prophecy, and he knew he said it as much for himself as for Amber. The words meant survival.

- 20 -

1100 HOURS - ZERO DAY +9

LUIS "SPYDER" ACOSTA, gang boss of West Cumberland and North 33rd, paced back and forth outside some anonymous shit-brown tent and glared at the emblem on the flag next to its entry. The big red star with a golden wreath around it was fuckin' stupid, but at least it wasn't that squiggly worm the ragheads used for a symbol. Nearby, Sebastian squatted on his heels, relaxed but poised, and watchful as always.

"Who the hell are these bitches," Spyder complained for perhaps the tenth time. "Nobody summons King Spyder. I came 'cuz I'm curious, but I'm about to bounce out."

Sebastian showed no expression in response, but said, "Boss, you gotta chill. I think these guys are calling shots for the ragheads. I'll bust 'em if you want, but I don't think we'd make it out, and they might make better friends than enemies. Let's see what they got to say and then decide what to do. Yeah?"

"Fuck you, Seb. I know that, dipshit. Aw hell, I'm too wound up. I gotta chill. I ain't even mad at you, yo, I'm just letting off steam. So who you think they are?"

"Who, the red star guys? I dunno, boss. But they got mad reps. You see how there ain't no more tents around this one? It's like an island. I bet you're in here to meet their Jeffe."

"Shit, then I better quiet down, yo. I just hate waiting." Spyder resumed pacing.

Ten minutes later, some short little slant-eyed dude came out wearing the ugliest uniform ever. Spyder straightened himself up and raised his chin. "What's up, yo?"

The little man stood stiffly, but Spyder couldn't read the little rice-eater's face. They all looked the same. Then the little puto said, "Mister Spyder, you have the honor of being summoned to meet with Colonel Ree of the Korean People's Army. You may say he is in command of this area. Your recent activities have gained his admiration, but also his attention. When you speak to him, you must call him 'Colonel' or 'Sir' only. Colonel Ree is a great man, a man of power and wisdom. All the People cheer his name and honor the Great Leader for bringing him here. Do you understand the nature of the man you will soon meet?"

Spyder suppressed the urge to laugh at this little dipshit's stupid accent and the garbage he was spouting. Who the fuck cheers a gook's name? Ree was probably shorter than this puto and just as ugly. "Yeah, I get it. This is your house, your rules. When do we meet Colonel?"

"Follow me," said the little man and stepped back into the tent through the loose flap.

Spyder shrugged and followed, Sebastian close on his heels. When they got inside, it took a moment for Spyder's eyes to adjust. The first thing he noticed were the colonel's two guards. These didn't look like just any old goose-steppers. No, they were poised, wary, and oozed menace. And yet, the colonel himself didn't look like much. Not too short, but not tall, and thin. He sat on a simple folding chair with a large, expensive-looking rug laid out before him.

"I am Colonel Ree," the skinny slant told Spyder. "Please be seated, and be at ease. I will not harm you here, so long as you show this place the respect I feel it deserves." Spyder had a hard time following the translator, who spoke almost on top of the colonel. Then the translator said, "Please do not look at me. That honor is the colonel's. I merely translate."

Spyder nodded, and he and Sebastian squatted on their heels a safe distance from the colonel. "Tell him I'm glad to meet him. What's he want?"

The translator spoke in Korean, and the colonel let out a laugh. Spyder had the distinct impression that the colonel laughed only to show his guards that he wasn't insulted enough to order throats slit.

Ree said, "I wish to congratulate you on your victory over your southern neighbor. You enlarge your territory at the expense of your enemy, and your resources now increase. But, so do your responsibilities."

Spyder's eyes narrowed. "We been doing what we're told, Colonel. Kill peeps with guns, kill or catch soldiers, and two slaves a day, in return for food and supplies. Seems like it's all good, yeah?"

"Your people have now almost doubled. So, I will double your allotments. You will continue to flush out Resistance sympathizers, and your quota of 'volunteer workers' is doubled. Four per day—and they must not be infirm or under the age of thirteen. I need workers, not more mouths to feed."

"Well, I don't want them slackers either, Colonel. What do you want me to do? I gotta get rid of them somehow."

The colonel smiled. "Do with them as you will. I do not care how you handle them. Just do not send them to me."

Spyder nodded. "Anything else, sir?" He practically spat the word, hating it, but it was necessary.

"I am done with you, my excellent servant," replied Colonel Ree, returning Spyder's gaze coldly.

Spyder wanted to scratch the bastard's eyes out. That tone he used would have been the death of any other man, but here Spyder was, king of his own territory, eating crap sandwiches for this little slant-eye.

Spyder stood without another word and walked out of the tent with as much calm as he could muster, and then he and Sebastian headed home. "Some day I'm gonna kill that puto," Spyder muttered under his breath.

"Better do it before he gets to asking for more than he already is. We got the guns to run over this place if you want."

"You're a fool, Seb," Spyder said with a grin. "Don't you know they got a whole army here? We gotta do it Godfather-style, no links. Make it look like someone else."

"Whatever you say, boss. Seems like long odds to me, but you in charge, yo."

Spyder looked at Sebastian, but his face was expressionless. "I am in charge, puto. You need another knife in you to remember that?"

Sebastian shuddered but said nothing and Spyder whistled a happy tune as the two men walked out of the camp.

* * *

Mandy stood with the adults of the clan in a semicircle around the newly-turned earth, with Kaitlyn wrapped in her mother's arms as they faced the grave. Now buried, Jed would feel no more pain or fear, but his wife and daughter certainly could, and both were crying. Jaz too was crying, though she had the good sense to stand back a little and let this be a time for the man's family. Mandy and her family didn't have a strong connection to Jed, but there had been no question whether they'd attend—in this new world, *the clan was the family*. They all felt it, and Frank sometimes said it aloud like a mantra. *We are a clan.*

Standing next to her mother, Cassy muttered, "I want to kill every goddamn one of those bastards."

Mandy realized the comment wasn't to her or anyone else in particular. Her daughter likely had just spoken her thoughts out loud. Still, Mandy was irritated. "Sweetie, don't take the Lord's name in vain. I raised you better."

"Really, Mom, you want to have this conversation now?"

"What better time? The Lord should be on our minds. Jed's body is gone, but his soul is free. It's sad for us and for his family, but a time of joy for Jed as he sits at the table of the Lord." Without waiting for a response, Mandy stepped forward. "Amber, may I say a few words?"

Amber nodded, and Mandy brought her hands together and bowed her head. The others followed her example. Ethan looked self-conscious but went along with it.

"O God, by whose mercy the faithful departed find rest, look kindly on Your departed son who gave his life in the service of his country and his clan. Grant that, through the death and resurrection of Your only-begotten Son, he may share in the joy of Your Heavenly Kingdom and rejoice in You with your saints forever. Father God, though Jed is at peace now, and we thank You, we ask that You guide and strengthen those of us who remain in this fallen world. Lord, let not his sacrifice be in vain and as we face the minions of evil, Lord, be our aim, be our strength, and let us at last overcome, so that we Your people might not perish from the earth. We ask this in the name of Jesus Christ. Amen."

The others muttered "Amen" in response and then stepped away respectfully, leaving Amber and Kaitlyn to say their own final goodbyes.

As Mandy and Cassy walked away toward their temporary camp, Mandy stopped and turned to her. "Cassy, sweetie, listen. I know you and Jasmine have had issues, but she's a young woman. Seen from my age, she might as well still be a child, and she's a child who hurts more than you may realize. You know how it feels to lose someone you love. Please, for me, will you be kind to her for a few days? It costs nothing to be kind, and the Lord knew that when He said to turn the other cheek, it wasn't to help the wrongdoer. Forgiveness lightens the spirit of the one who was wronged. But if you can't do it because it's the right thing to do, then I ask you, please just do it as a favor for me."

Cassy stared at her for a few seconds, but Mandy's gaze never wavered. Right was right, and God knew what He was doing when He gave His inspired Word to the world. Mandy wasn't brave, but she stood strong in her faith. Cassy wasn't going to make her waver. She steeled herself for her daughter's response.

To her surprise, however, Cassy finally nodded. "You're right, Mom. She's part of the clan, and so am I. I'll put my own issues aside, at least for now. I've been rethinking anyway, based on how she's behaved in the clan so far. Learning and working hard. So Amber and Jaz both need support, and the clan can't afford any squabbling right now. But Mom, worry more about Kaitlyn than Jaz, okay? Jaz is a survivor."

* * *

Ethan wanted desperately to comfort Amber, but he knew this was the wrong time for it. The clan had to heal before he could hope to forge a new connection with her. He was surprised at how much that realization hurt, but it was necessary. Besides, what the hell could he say to her? He had no idea how to comfort people. The closest to death he'd ever been was making mock speeches over the body of a fallen comrade during some castle raid online, waiting for the "departed" to respawn.

Worse yet, he was having a hard time looking at anyone in the group. Every time someone looked at him it made his skin get bumps, and he imagined that they somehow knew. Knew how Jed really died, knew what a liar and a coward he was. Oh sure, he'd crept forward with a grenade, but at the time, it was either do that or die. Well, there was also the time in his house when he'd come to their rescue—but again, it was either that or risk losing his bunker before he was ready. He had only done what was needful.

Why couldn't life be more like a video game? No risk, all reward, and if he messed up he could just wait for a new Instance and try the mission again. Online he was a bona fide hero; here he was overweight and had more ideas than skills.

A flash of irritation washed over him. Life was unfair, always had been. Screw it, he thought, it was time for a walk. He shoved hands in his pockets and, head down, began to wander toward what was left of the ambush site. Maybe looking at dead invaders would make him feel better. Or, at least distract him. One foot in front of the other, he slowly made his way to the trees and to the emplacement, and simply stood looking down at the carnage. No one bothered to bury these bastards, and he damn sure wasn't going to. Leave their cursed jihadist bones for the coyotes, or whatever predators ran around here. He spat down into the carnage.

As he stood there, the entire scene replayed itself in his head, over and over. Deep inside, he knew he'd felt something like a ferocious joy when Jed had been shot, and again when Ethan's own grenade flew true to the entrenchment of the ambushers. Before it had even landed, he knew it would finish off Jed and tried to scream a warning, but inside Ethan knew he had felt glad at first. The guilt of that flash of emotion during the ambush now made him want to vomit. How the hell could he *want* Jed to die? What the hell was he thinking, what kind of man did that?

"I didn't kill you, Jed," he whispered, and knew it was true—the two gut shots would have been the end of Jed anyway—but it didn't make him feel better about the instant of raw, savage joy he'd felt at the prospect of Jed dying, his fault or not. Now he couldn't even look at Amber without being flooded with feelings he was just not yet able to deal with.

Ethan heard a snap of twigs to his left and spun, raising his M4, but what he saw stopped him just short of firing by reflex. Two men and a woman were crouched aside nearby trees, and they carried M4s, not pointed at him but definitely at the ready if they needed to fire.

"Put that rifle away, citizen," said the larger of the two men, and though he hadn't shouted, his voice was piercing in that way that Michael did sometimes.

As Ethan's mind caught up, he began to see details. M4 rifles and they were wearing military BDUs, the camouflage field uniforms of soldiers. No, not soldiers—Marines, he amended when he saw the distinctive "eagle, globe, and anchor" emblem of the USMC on their hats. Covers, Michael called them.

"Where the hell did you come from," Ethan blurted, but carefully lowered his own rifle. Best not to get shot by American Marines, yeah.

"Training camp in Raleigh," the Marine grunted. "Who the hell are you people?"

The sound of a rifle being racked came from nearby, and Ethan saw in his peripheral vision that Michael had crept up, and now had them covered with his own weapon.

"Oorah, jarheads! Set those rifles down real slow," barked Michael.

Ethan felt certain that if they refused, he was going to spray all three of them. They must have read it in him too because they followed his instructions immediately.

"We're not the enemy, civilian," said the burly Marine.

"Shit's real FUBAR right now, d-dawgs, and I don't know anything about you. You said you came from Raleigh? That's a training center, not a base. Yet you're in full field gear. Explain yourselves, Staff Sergeant," instructed Michael.

Ethan had missed the ranks, but looked now and saw that the larger man was indeed an E-6 while the other man was an E-2 or Private First Class, and the woman was an E-3 Lance Corporal. Michael had only been a sergeant, and Ethan wasn't sure about his duty status. Shit.

"Ten went out to screw around in the woods and get drunk on leave. Three remain after trying to get back into Raleigh, and failing. We did get a bunch of gear, though, mostly with us in the trunks of our cars, but we got more ammo off some National Guards guys we found all shot up. Then we bugged out using some working Hummers until they ran out of gas. And here we are."

Michael stared at them for a long while, and Ethan had the strong impression he was examining every detail of their uniforms, and the gear they carried. But finally, Michael lowered his rifle and straightened up, rolling his shoulders around to loosen them. "Very well, Marines. What are your standing orders, if any?"

"Executive Orders are for Martial Law with the doctrines for operating in enemy-occupied American territory."

Michael spat. "Shove Martial Law up your ass, jarhead. We may qualify as partisans, but you can bet your REMF asses that we aren't taking any orders from you, and you're a damn fool to bring it up."

The Marine shrugged. "We'll see. For now, this is your rodeo. But I got your number—you're military. Name, rank and serial number. Please." Ethan was certain the Marine was making no mere request.

"Bates, Michael K., Sergeant, USMC Retired, 555-55-5555, numbnuts."

The Marine grinned. "You're too young to be retired, and anyway, guess what? We're at war and I just re-drafted you."

Frank's voice sounded out then, loud and clear, along with the sound of a round going into his rifle chamber, "Mister, we just left one of our own and ten of *them* here in this dirt, and I'm not above leaving three more. Michael's with us, and if you don't like it, you can go fill out a report in triplicate, and then shove it up your ass."

The woman slowly set her rifle down, then stood with her palms up and out to her side. "Hey, hey. We're getting off on the wrong foot. You lost someone, you said? Well, we lost *seven* of our boys and girls. They died well, but they're still dead, and maybe our tensions are all a little high, right? So let's just calm down."

The Staff Sgt. raised an eyebrow as he looked to the lance corporal, but he didn't interrupt her. She continued, "What we're really doing, or what our mission priority really is or should be, is to find a place to hole up and go guerrilla. The normal rules went out the window when my cell phone died, I think. So let's figure this out together, okay?"

Frank slowly moved his open left hand in a low, flat swing toward Michael. "Stand down, Michael. I don't want to have to shoot Americans, and I sure don't want them shooting at us. Okay, lady, you got more sense than your pencil-pushing leader over there, so from now on, we'll talk to you, and he can go fill out Form 240-fuck-all."

Ethan fought down the urge to grin. Damn, but Frank had some balls on him! Thank God he'd saved this guy back at the bunker...

Michael lowered his rifle but kept it in a ready position. "Sure thing, Frank. You're the boss. They're just following procedure. Rear-Echelon bull crap, but still procedure. Well, S.O.P. doesn't apply, Marines, got it?"

The lead Marine shrugged and looked to the woman. "Your show, Lance Corporal."

She nodded and looked back at Michael. "You got blood on your leg, Marine. Want me to take a look? I used to be a paramedic."

Michael shook his head and glanced to Frank. Ethan saw Frank's jaw clench and unclench, a sure sign the boss was pretty amped up. But "boss"? When did that happen, was there a memo? Well okay, why not, everybody treated him as their leader anyway...

Frank said, "So you got full loads of ammo, food, all that? We aren't a charity, but we'll do what we can to help Americans."

"No need, we're loaded up. We had lots of casualties to restock from," she replied, and her eyes narrowed when she said the last part. Ethan could understand just how she must feel, and thought of Jed again with a jolt of pain he couldn't get used to.

"Alright, come on down. Meet the others. But if you try any B.S. we're going to be a lot less friendly, you get my drift?"

The woman nodded to Frank. "Affirmative. You refuse to be in the proper chain of command but aren't hostile. Yet. We'll behave. Right, Sarge?"

The burly man nodded. "I'm Mueller, the lance corporal is Sturm, and the quiet guy is PFC Martinez, though he looks more Irish than Mexican."

"Argentina, Sarge. Still Argentina."

Mueller grinned. "That's why your tacos suck, Martinez."

The group trudged down toward the clan's temporary camp, Michael and Frank in the rear and Ethan leading them. Ethan got the distinct impression this was so they could shoot these Marines if they did anything stupid, and he was again thankful they got Frank as their leader. Boss. Whatever.

As they approached, Ethan heard Cassy's voice, saying, "...and we're just a hop, skip and a jump from the homestead. This nightmare will be over in a few hours."

Then everyone grew silent when they saw the others returning with three unknown faces. Frank spoke up loudly, and said, "These are three lost Marines. They want to kill invaders and chew bubblegum, but they're out of bubblegum. I think we should bring 'em with us, Cassy, if you've got the room and supplies. They've agreed to be good little guests."

SSgt. Mueller spoke up. "Absolutely. We need a base of operations, and you folks could clearly use a few more guns. Maybe we can make a deal."

Ethan's heart leapt at that. Amber would be safer with Marines, and the woman, Sturm, had medical training. With the homestead only hours away now, they could use more hands on the farm, too. Win-win-win all around.

Cassy smiled. "We've suffered losses, but now we gain new friends. God's blessing us right now, if we have the wisdom to see it—or that's what my mom would say—and if you can't trust Marines, who can you trust?"

Ethan saw her glance to Michael as she said that, and then she began introducing everyone. He just hoped her instincts were right to trust these people, just as they had been right to trust Frank and his people. Yeah, it all would work out. It had to.

- 21 -

1600 HOURS - ZERO DAY +9

THE CLAN TRUDGED for hours, and with every step Cassy's arm hurt less, and her heart raced more. Home was so close she could almost taste it. And despite all the odds against them, they'd come so far with only one loss. In a way, the loss of Jed solved a possible problem with Amber, but Cassy would have rather had Jed alive and well and, despite lingering issues with Jaz, Cassy knew the pain she was feeling. Frank said Jed was a wiz with machines and what he called "redneck ingenuity," and that kind of horse sense would have been invaluable to the group.

The three Marine newcomers mostly kept to themselves, taking the left flank as the group traveled, which freed up others to help with the kids, and so the whole group had moved faster. That was damn convenient, even if she didn't really believe the new Marines could have the clan's interests at heart. Still, they'd insisted on coming and, short of shooting American Marines, there was little reason for the clan to stop them. At least they seemed like okay people—but she still wouldn't trust them any time soon, and Frank had told her that he felt much the same. That made her feel at least a little less tense about their presence.

Mandy must have been thinking in the same direction as Cassy because in a private moment with Cassy she blurted, "I guess as long as we convince them their interests are the same as ours they'll be useful to have around."

"Who, the Marines? Their interests *are* the same as ours, so long as they don't try to commandeer our supplies or act like they own the place. It's my home, and they'll have to respect it or leave."

They reached the top of a small rise and looked down into a lush little valley. Cassy's eyes watered, and she grinned from ear to ear. "Look, Mom... Home. And the bastards didn't spray it. The windmills are still working. And see all those trees to the north side? Those are all either fruit or nut trees, or dwarf breeds to draw birds to enrich the soil and control pests. And all that underbrush you see isn't weeds; they're berries and fruit and veggies, mostly, but a lot are just there to fertilize the soil, or medicinal. Lots of comfrey. Those three sparkling jewels down there are my fish ponds. The water runs from the top of the hills north, down to the first pond, which overflows to the second, and so on. Those sheds are for smoking meat, solar dehydrators, and so on."

"What are the ripples, dear? Your hillside looks like it has wrinkles all over."

"Those are swales and berms. Ditches that collect rain water and slowly soak it into the soil. On the downhill side from each ditch is a mound, with dead wood at the bottom and covered over in soil and cover crops, bushes, dwarf tree breeds... I could go a whole year without rain, and my land would stay green, there's so much water in the soil."

Mandy smiled. "Impressive. I've been here before, but I'm seeing different things now. As the Lord says, we must be good caretakers of the earth and its bounty. I never really thought of your prepping that way, but I guess I was a bit narrow-minded."

"Just stuck in your ways, Mom. Most of being prepared means being *resilient*, so you can adapt to changes as they come. But it goes on from there, Mom. The pigs, for example, eat whatever falls off the trees that I don't gather up, which fattens them up, and they leave their droppings behind to enrich the soil. Everything here is connected to everything else in one way or another. If you look, you can see God's plan for the world in miniature, here."

"And you have guns, too, I imagine," Mandy said with a smile. She was teasing, of course, but Cassy decided to accept it at face value for now. Nothing was going to screw up her mood today. "Yeah, for hunting and defense. They're just tools, Mom. Use them wisely and they help, but use them badly at your own peril."

"And those things moving around up on the hillside above the house?"

"Two goats for milk and cheese, four sheep for wool, and the four pigs. They all live up there on the lee side so any wastes I don't gather to compost will work their way downhill on their own when it rains."

"Think they're all still alive? You haven't been home in a while."

"Eleven days. They should be okay. Their water is gravity fed, and the cistern up there was full when I left. Water gets pumped into it from the first pond by a solar pump, which must be fried now. But I have a manual pumping system for backup. Windmill power, too, with a little conversion work. The animals are probably damn hungry by now, though."

Michael interrupted their conversation. "Cassy, should anyone be there at the farm? I'm going to recon it before we all walk down there like lambs to a slaughter, if bad guys are holed up there."

"No, nobody belongs there now. Recon's a good idea, Mike." She smiled at him.

Michael turned on his heels and strode toward the farm, bearing east of it to come in from a flank side. Cassy let out a contented sigh, and sat down to watch, and to answer the million questions the others, like her mom, were just starting to ask.

Tiffany sat roughly down next to Cassy and gazed out over the farm. "Where's the septic tank? You got the whole half acre around the house covered entirely in raised beds. Don't you need a drain field?"

Cassy laughed. "That's a weird question. But if you're asking if you have to use an outhouse, the answer is no. Normal toilets, ultra-low flush ones, that unload into a cistern buried flush with the ground right outside the bathroom wall. Lots of worms in there, which eat the wastes about as quickly as you can put them in. The liquid—urine, worm tea, whatever—drains down through a pipe and into a series of wet-water channels with swampy-type plants. Three sets of channels, in series. The plants filter the water almost completely before it drains down into the lower fish pond. And the overflow from the fish pond, with all those nutrients, gets diverted through the little forest you see down there. No waste, and you don't have to pump out outhouses. Pretty slick, really."

"That's gross. But, as long as I can poop inside like a normal human, I'll overlook it." Tiffany shared a laugh with Cassy over that.

"Everything is going to take getting used to, Tiff. But I have kids, and I wasn't trying to be some Lone Ranger mountain man type. I just like being prepared for things, and in the meantime, it's a healthy, happy way to live. And truth be told, I feel like it's a lifestyle that puts me closer in touch with my mom's God, though I have my doubts about Him.

Don't tell Mandy I said that. But we'll be fine here, Tiff. You, your kids, all of us. We're *home*."

A short time later, Michael returned wearing a grin. "All clear," he announced. "Looks like a cow has been slaughtered, and there's no food in the cabinets."

Cassy pursed her lips. "So someone was there?"

"Yeah," replied Michael, "but they're not there now. The fireplace is warm, and there's a cast iron kettle over it, also warm. Whoever was there, it was recent. But I scouted the whole place, briefly, and saw no sign of anyone there now."

Cassy's heart soared. "Home," she said with a lopsided grin. Home again, home for the kids, and for the clan. A chance to regroup and to live. Not just survive, but really live. "Let's get going," she said with her voice raised almost into a song.

* * *

Peter's eyes bulged when he saw where the spy was heading. His experienced eyes made out so many tiny little details, like the placement of animal pens and the water infiltration mounds, that his head swam. It was all too labor intensive for the kind of farming he'd done, but he understood the beauty and simplicity of the system. He sat down and began taking page after page of notes on ideas he got from the farm, and sketching out a map.

Better yet, on the far side of the hill the farm was on, there stretched miles and miles of forest. Government land... Sure to be full of game. To either side of her farm were other farms, though they looked more like what he expected a small farm to look like. Well, he'd have the manpower to convert those farms to the way the spy did things, when he led his people to this Promised Land. And heck, they would even be able to use the people who lived there now to do most of the hard, dangerous work. Wouldn't *that* make his followers happy?

The only downside was the damn soldiers the spy picked up along the way. Those three looked like they knew their shit. Maybe he could find a way to contact them, make a deal, before he took over this oasis. That could be risky, though. It might blow the surprise. He'd have to mull that over for a while. Probably he'd just have to make sure they died first. Easy enough with a surprise attack, if he could get his scouts to sit still long enough for the targets of opportunity to present themselves all at once. Then if he put the rest of his shooters up at the crest of the hill on the north side of the house they could lay fire down onto them, and from elevation. Yeah, that might work. Surprise, surprise, bitch.

After he was done taking notes, he gathered his things and, with a heavy sigh at the thought of the journey ahead of him, began the trudge back home, or to whatever was left of it after the invaders bombed it. He'd get his revenge, surely, and better yet he'd found a home for all of his people. All the women, the children, his friends—no more of them would have to die, once they'd taken over and settled in. For the first time in a week, he had a strong sense of confidence. His people would make it. And he would lead them to this Promised Land.

- 22 -

0600 HOURS - ZERO DAY +10

CASSY STRETCHED, BUMPING into Brianna next to her, and it took a moment for her mind to realize where she was. *Home.* She sat up and rubbed her eyes. The room was stuffed, with Bri and Aidan in bed with her, plus Frank and Mary and their kid scattered all around on the floor. The upstairs second bedroom, she remembered, was equally stuffed with Michael, Tiffany, their kids and the three Marines. The living room slept the rest of the party, mostly on the floor. Well, she'd have to figure out something soon, because this was just too many people for her two-bedroom house. If a fire broke out, or if they were attacked, they'd be tripping all over each other. An attack was certainly possible and not only by the invaders. That was a sobering thought.

Cassy made her way through the house, waking the adults. It wasn't difficult to wake them; they were all accustomed to rising with the sun now. Not much light got into the house yet, but their body clocks were set. Soon the house was awake, everyone had gone through the line to use the one bathroom, and Cassy had assembled them all outside. Looking around, it was clear the clan was more relaxed than they'd been since she met them. Today promised to be a good day, despite the amount of work that needed doing.

With Frank standing beside her, she told the clan what chores needed doing first thing in the morning, and that breakfast would be around 8:00 a.m. The kids were assigned to feed the animals and gather the eggs from her chickens and from the ducks at the ponds, with Brianna given the task of supervising it all. Bri had done it many times before on her own, of course, but Cassy wanted them all to know how. Brianna rolled her eyes but didn't argue. Cassy suppressed a smile. Her daughter would probably roll her eyes if she won a million bucks. Teenagers, hah.

"Michael, you're now head of security. Take the Marines and wander around the property. Look for anything wrong, of course, but mostly I think it'd be good if you were familiar with every inch of this place, and can identify any security risks. Even here, people will be hungry, and we have a lot of food around for the taking—that little forest I have is mostly food, not natural woods. It just looks like woods. But my neighbors probably know it's really a 'food forest,' so we should at least know where they're likely to come in from, if anyone gets ideas."

Mandy frowned and said, "Cassy, you should have more faith in your fellow man. God put us here for a reason, and He won't let us stumble now. Faith, hope, and love, and the greatest of these is love."

Cassy nodded in agreement. "Of course, Mom. In fact, I had made a lot of friends among my neighbors, and after we get settled in we'll be going to find them, and invite them into the homestead. Mutual protection and more skills, and all that. But it's prudent to at least be prepared for trouble. Okay, Michael, you and the Marines can go anywhere and everywhere. Eventually, you'll want to put some security measures in place, I imagine, and I'll support whatever decision you make so long as it doesn't cut into our food production, so be thinking long-term security."

Michael nodded and signaled the three Marines. When they had departed, she was left with Jaz, Mandy, Frank, Tiffany, Mary and Amber, as well as Ethan. "Mom, would you please take everyone but Frank and Ethan with you to the outdoor kitchen? Get them familiar with how everything works, how to light the rocket stoves, where the utensils are and so on?"

Amber cocked her head to one side. "What's a rocket stove, Cassy? Is it safe?"

Cassy grinned and said, "It's just a wood-burning stove that uses about a quarter of the fuel of other stoves. Bits of wood, even twigs, go into an opening toward the bottom and because of the chimney on the other side, the draft it creates makes the fire roar like a rocket. It burns clean, too, so once it gets good and hot, there's not even any smoke on the other side. I have two, one that heats a cast iron griddle and one that has covers you can remove to use frying pans, Dutch ovens and so on. Both stoves vent around an enclosed chamber you can use as an oven, too. Mandy will show you all the details. She's cooked here before."

At last she was left with only Ethan and Frank, who looked at her with amusement. "Quite the queen bee, Cass," Frank chuckled.

Cassy nodded without smiling. "This is a working farm. There's work to do, and everything here is done a lot differently than any farm you've probably seen. Putting it all together was sort of a hobby, but I'm glad now I caught the 'prepper bug.' *You* are the clan leader, Frank, I know that. But until I'm positive that everyone knows how to do everything there is to do here, I'm going to have my hands full teaching. I'm glad Mandy and Brianna already know enough to handle some of the teaching, and Michael and the jarheads know more about combat readiness and security than I ever will. But, enough." She finally smiled. "I have something to show you guys that's gonna blow your mind." Her smile broadened to a huge, mischievous grin that made both Ethan and Frank grin back at her in anticipation.

As they stood in the living room, Cassy gave a dramatic bow, then casually reached down to the bottom step on the staircase, and lifted. Much of the staircase rose, swiveling on hidden hinges halfway up the flight, and revealed another staircase going down into darkness. Frank drew a sudden breath, and Ethan wore a big sloppy grin as soon as he realized what she'd put together.

"This," said Cassy, "is the hidden way into my Fortress of Solitude. I didn't want those Marines to see it yet, but I had to share it with you guys. We've work to do down there, so let's get cracking."

Cassy led them downward, producing a flashlight to light the way. The stairs went down about ten feet, then turned right to go down another ten feet or so, and ended in a heavy-looking steel door with a large metal circular handle in the center. Next to the door was a keypad with metal buttons, and between the keypad and the door was a thick metal lever.

"Mechanical, not electronic," Cassy muttered and typed in several numbers, and she heard the faint sounds of pushrods sliding inside channels. Then she lifted the lever, producing a heavy thunk, and spun the handle. With a grunt she swung the door outward toward herself, stepping around it as it opened. She stepped inside and pushed a button next to the door on the inside wall, and lights came on, one after the other, illuminating a bunker in a soft glow. Honest to goodness electric lighting.

"Twelve volt lighting, off batteries. This whole bunker is a giant Faraday cage."

Ethan laughed out loud, then. "Amazing. How do you charge them? Didn't the EMP take out the system?"

"Nope. I have a manual disconnect between the panels and the charge controller, with several surge suppressors and TVSs—transient voltage suppressors—in line with the controller. I disconnect it when I'm away, and I have two spares for everything. What that means for us is, once I flip the switch back on, my solar panels on the roof will start working again. Everything's 12-volt here, or uses alternative power, so it's enough juice for what little was electronic here—TVs, laptops, cell phones, lights, and a slew of battery-powered tools in the work shed."

Frank let out a low whistle. "We're in business, Cassy. You're a godsend. Whatever made you do all this?"

Ethan answered for her. "Because she wanted to be prepared for the kind of crap that just happened. They called me crazy, too, but we're all alive because I'm crazy. And we'll stay alive because Cassy here is a nut job, too."

Cassy laughed too, then. "No, I really thought it was going to be a collapse of the dollar, not an EMP, but I figured if I just got ready for a zombie apocalypse then all the other stuff-hit-the-fan scenarios would be covered, too. Plus, people don't look at you so funny if you say you're prepping for zombies. Tell them the dollar will collapse and they call you a nut, but laugh and tell them it's for zombies, and they just think you're an eccentric hobbyist. Better eccentric than crazy. And I designed the whole place to look more like a retreat than a working farm, with the food forest and all. Actually, that might have saved it from being sprayed with that brown gunk, come to think of it."

Ethan said, "So what all do you have down here? Rations, communications, medical, or what?"

"This bunker is made of five buried and reinforced forty-foot shipping containers. They needed reinforcement because, as I found out, if you just bury a cargo container it can buckle from the weight overhead. Anyway, the five containers are all interconnected. One is a sleeping bay, like on a submarine, with eighteen berths and tons of shelves. One holds my firearms, chemicals, electronics—including two HAM radios and a dozen handheld radios—and other miscellaneous crap. The third and fourth ones hold enough food for the whole clan for probably a couple years, if we ration it. And we're in the fifth one, a living space and communications center. Two side tunnels lead to hidden escapes around the farm."

Frank grunted. "What did that set you back?"

Cassy shrugged. "Money's worthless now, of course, but when my husband died he left enough to get the farm mostly finished, and to put in my bunker. I think getting the containers and placing them came in under fifty thousand, and I had a lot more than that. The rest I spent on finishing out the bunker's features and completing the farm, like getting the swales and berms dug in, the windmills and solar installed, the HAM radios set up. I have five each of .22 rifles, .308 rifles, AR-15s, 12-gauge shotguns, and .40-caliber pistols, along with some crossbows and about ten thousand rounds of ammo for each type of gun. Backpacks, med-kits, extra pots and pans, wool blankets, bathroom incidentals. Even a small prepper and intensive farming book collection. The works. Enough for all of us, and for the neighbors I'll be inviting in—the ones I've made friends with and know they'll be a good fit, and will contribute something to the group."

Ethan looked Cassy in the eyes, and in a pleading voice said, "Please tell me you remembered to set up an antenna for the HAMs..."

"I do have one plus a spare, but we'll have to set it up.

We'll also have to set up the solar panel system, get it checked out, and tie in the backup windmill generator. That isn't hard, so we can get that done after breakfast. Anybody hungry?"

* * *

1000 HOURS - ZERO DAY +10

Why couldn't this be as easy as crafting items in his online games, Ethan groaned as he tested his setup. The HAM antenna was in place, and he'd spent the last hour in the living room getting his programs installed on the laptop Cassy gave him. Soon he'd be ready to broadcast again, and also to connect to his hidden satellite connection. He was eager to see if the 20s had sent him anything since the last time he'd connected. One last test was running on the laptop before he'd consider it ready.

There was a noise from the computer, a "job finished" beep, and Ethan smiled to see that everything checked out. He was ready to go. He clicked on a desktop icon of an antenna, bringing up his comms program suite. He'd written most of the code himself. He watched with satisfaction as his backdoor satellite link connected, then ran a series of searches for VPNs around the world, many of which had been installed by malware on the PCs of unsuspecting people.

Most of his pre-EMP connections were greyed out, no longer operational. Still, within a few minutes he'd found six around the world, and stopped the program. Then he clicked another button, and the graphic display showed his satellite connection bouncing from one VPN to the next, a chain of links that would make it nearly impossible to track him in the time he'd be online. In a few seconds, the graphic display of the network changed from pulsing red to solid green. Show time.

The now-familiar dialog box opened on his screen after the last connection was made, and showed only one message.

> *Attn: Dark Ryder - Update and Instructions*
> *Well done, DR. We see you have stopped moving in an ideal location for a base of operations. Advise if this is final location. Attached is a file to download latest data for broadcasting. Be advised, satellites show few enemy patrols in the region. Intel says area deemed too sparsely populated/farmed to be of interest at this stage. However, at least two groups numbering approx. 20 each active in the area. Base camps appear to be east and west of your current loc. in forest to north. They are confirmed raiding local homesteads/houses for supplies. Taking people back to basecamp. Suspect for sustenance, as victims not visible on next satellite pass. Good luck.*

Ethan cringed. Could things really be that bad out there already? Yes, he supposed they could. By the Rules of Three, people could only survive about three weeks without food and even accounting for most peoples' pantries, the food had been gone for a week. That was a long time to go without food. Not fatal, but not everyone was going to let their kids go hungry for a week when human "long pig" was everywhere for the taking. Disgusting. The good news was that there weren't many enemy soldiers in the area. That was something, at least.

He replied in the dialog box,

> *DR responding. Confirm location final. Thanks for intel update. Will grok attachment and broadcast later.*

Need to figure out how to broadcast without drawing enemy attention to location.

The response came quickly.

> DR: We ack. Fear not. Solution ready. We have several repeaters set up in your region; will pick up sig and bounce them around. Enemy will not know which one. They'll eventually check out all of them, recommend relocate to broadcast then bugout, change loc each broadcast. Avoid pattern such as circle around base. Notify us and receive ack 5 min before each broadcast so we can bring them up. Please ack.

Ethan acknowledged, and then the window closed on its own; his 20s contact must have closed the connection remotely. So, he could broadcast in relative safety, but would only be able to do it a few times before they pinned down which one was the live connection, just by process of elimination. If he broadcast too many times they'd probably send a drone to blow him up, and that would be the end of transmission. Worse, he'd only know when he'd hit that magic number when he saw a drone-launched missile rocketing toward his face. Super.

Ethan pulled up the file attachment, decoded it, and began reading. It was in the same format as before, listing enemy unit, estimated manpower, location as of last broadcast, and current last known location. That was followed by a list of supply cache coordinates, along with the categories and quantities of supplies each one contained.

At the end of the document was the intel summary. It seemed mostly the same; the enemy was solidifying control on the areas they already occupied and were struggling in New York and Florida though making headway despite significant casualty rates. Then something grabbed Ethan's attention: "*Operation Backdraft is a go.*" Whatever that meant. But if the 20s were coordinating an operation-level action, that could only be a good thing for America.

- 23 -

1300 HOURS - ZERO DAY +10

PETER RAN ON foot. He'd been eating a lunch of freshly-foraged berries and plants when a group of nearly two dozen people stumbled onto him.

Peter slowed to a walk and cursed himself a fool for letting them sneak up on him. It wasn't really his own fault, he fumed. He was tired and foggy-headed from not eating enough the last few days. Not for the first time he wished he still had the horse he'd left the Farms with, but at least he had his important gear in his backpack, along with his notebook, and he'd grabbed his rifle.

It occurred to him that perhaps he'd made a mistake letting his scout companions go home without him. It would be a dangerous journey, and some extra muscle would be nice. Water under the bridge, though. Now he had to get home fast, and the faster, the better. He decided to take the road, trading safety for speed. He hoped the hungry mobs had given up on the roads by now, and his way would be mostly clear.

He came upon a large road, Highway 322, which would take him south all the way to West Chester, close to home.

Fifty miles to go. A quick calculation with his most recent pace count told him it would take about two full days to walk that far in his current state, but at least it would be on level ground, and fairly direct.

An hour later, still on the road, he trudged up a low hill. Reaching the crest, he looked ahead for any movement and then saw, at the base of the hill maybe a hundred yards away, a half-dozen people surrounding a red car. They were pounding on its windows, which were tinted to the point that Peter couldn't see into it. Near the car were a single sleeping bag and a backpack, but with the amount of debris scattered around it looked like the pack had been emptied. Peter didn't see any rifles among the attackers.

Damn it all, he'd have to either take a wide berth around that mess or go through it. And these assholes were probably attacking one unarmed person. Peter imagined the terror of whoever was hiding inside the abandoned car, and grew angry. The attackers were a bunch of unprepared animals, reduced to looting others who had prepared better just to survive. It wasn't right.

Peter muttered, "Okay, you vermin. I don't want to go around you, and whoever you're looting needs some help. I think I have the perfect, win-win solution. Sucks to be you bastards."

He raised his rifle and sighted in, adjusting for distance and elevation, glad he felt no wind. A burly male with a baseball bat, grinning savagely, was his first target. *Bang.* The man's neck spouted a geyser of blood, and he flopped over backwards. Peter quickly took aim at another, a woman, and she went down clutching her chest.

The others stared at the two people on the ground and looked confused, which made Peter grin as he dropped his third target, a skinny man wielding a knife. The remaining three ran from the road. Peter shot one in the back, and the last two sprinted out of view. Surprise was such a useful tool when dealing with problems like this.

Peter walked steadily down the hill, rifle at low ready but not directly aimed at the car, and came to within twenty feet before stopping. It was a beautiful car, he mused, an old Camaro that had been perfectly restored and painted bright red. He glanced at his watch—a quarter to four—and then stood still, simply looking at the car and waiting.

Five minutes later, a man stepped out of the car with a limp. He was of average height but muscular, with short hair and a goatee that stuck out past a scraggly, newly-growing beard. He wore a white t-shirt and jeans, with black boots, and he looked more cautious than scared.

Good, so he wasn't a coward. Peter would have hated to waste bullets saving a coward. "I'm Peter, and you're welcome." Peter kept his face carefully neutral. "Got yourself in a pickle, did you?"

"Yes, sir," said the man, also keeping his face unreadable. "I thank you for the help, mister. As you see, I don't have much to steal, if that's what you're about. My name's James, but my friends call me Jim."

"Nope. I just don't like to see people taking from strangers. Plus, they were in my way. Nice car. But, the lights went out over a week ago. Why on earth would you just sit here that long? You must've figured out help wasn't coming."

Jim scowled. "I've been here since last night. Where are you heading?"

Last night? That didn't add up. Peter said, "South, around West Chester. Sorry, I thought that was your car. It sure is nice, though."

"Well, mister, it is my car. I hid the keys, so don't think of taking it. I don't suppose you would, though. You had your chance to kill me already."

Peter felt a tingle race up his back. A working car... He

knew in theory that some cars must still run, but hadn't hoped to see one. An idea occurred to him. "Well, that's right. I could have, but I don't much care for murder unless a man deserves it. You've done me no wrong. But I reckon that means you have nowhere to go, or you'd be there."

Jim nodded slowly. "Yes. I've been driving around looking for a place to land, but everything is either burning or taken. And without a gun, I've had to escape trouble a couple of times in my car. I've stayed out of the towns, though. Too dangerous, and the pumps don't work anyway. I stopped here to siphon gas last night, and just didn't feel much like driving nowhere in particular today. I guess that was a mistake."

"When you stay put, people come across you. I had a horse this morning. Same situation as you, except they ate the horse and left me to run."

Jim grinned. "Well, Peter, I'll tell you what. If I give you a ride to wherever you're going, are you willing to ride shotgun and keep away the rabble? Maybe resupply me when we get there?

It was Peter's turn to smile. "Jim, that's a fine idea. But there's no need to resupply and send you on your way. I have people, a community. Give me a ride, and you'll earn a spot if you want it. They're good, hardworking people. You aren't coming in with your hand out, either. That car of yours is a meal ticket. And I give you my word, I won't let anyone take it from you. What do you say?"

Jim stood tall and limped up to Peter with his hand out. Shaking Peter's hand, he said, "That's a bargain, mister. I sure am glad you came along when you did. I don't know if I'll take you up on the community thing, but I'll give you that ride home. We'll see how things go from there. Sound fair?"

Yes, thought Peter, that sounded very fair indeed. Now instead of being two full days of walking through the chaos, the trip would only be a few hours. Even if they had to camp out for a night, he'd be home first thing in the morning. Peter smiled.

* * *

1600 HOURS - ZERO DAY +10

Ethan grunted as he set down the battery and inverter. Next to him, Amber gently set down his transmission rig. One of the Marines stood guard as he got down to business. Soon he had the flexible antenna set up, the radio plugged into the inverter, and connected the battery. He brought up his computer, plugged it into a Raspberry Pi module, and opened his translated and recoded file. Locking the "transmit" button into the on position, he clicked another icon and stood back as the coded broadcast went out on a loop.

Amber shook her head. "I have no idea what all that does, Ethan, but I hope these 20s guys make good use of whatever you're sending out."

Ethan grinned. "It's not the 20s who use it, but the various Resistance groups running around fighting the invaders, and some prepper compounds who participate some of the time. I have to imagine some of these Resistance groups were organized well before the EMPs went off, but that's not really my problem. I'm just one of a handful of agents who can do this work to keep the communications flowing as best we can."

"You've said all that before," Amber chuckled, and Ethan was glad to see her smile. She hadn't smiled much since Jed died.

Then the thought of Jed crashed into Ethan, and he cringed from the guilt he felt. He struggled to regain his composure, but Amber had seen the look.

"Yeah, I know. I miss Jed, but none of us think it's your fault. He went battle-mad, Michael says, and maybe he saved us but his death was his own fault. I never hated him, Ethan. I just hadn't been in love with him for a long time. He felt the same way."

Ethan shrugged. "Yeah, I know all that. I just wish I could have saved him. I was right there, and I felt powerless. I watched him die."

Amber put a hand on his arm. "You were powerless, Ethan, at least to save him. But you drew their fire so he could get close, when you missed with your grenade. We are alive because my husband died, and his kids at least get to know their father was a hero to us all. You are, too. You flanked them under fire, just like Jed. It could have worked out differently, but what happened is done. Life is what it is."

"So," Ethan began tentatively, "where does that leave you and me?"

"Nowhere, at the moment. You know I have feelings for you, Ethan. That hasn't changed. But Jed's kid deserve time to grieve before they see mommy with another man. Frank and Michael deserve that, too."

"But what do *you* deserve, Amber? Don't you deserve a fresh start? I think Jed was about to have 'the talk' with you about Jaz, from what I've heard. Just gossip, but it sounds right. He wanted to be happy. You deserve the same."

"Ethan, sweetie, listen. I do deserve to be happy, and so does everyone. But this is not the time for us. We can't be together right now. I don't know how long it'll take, but I know I have to wait. We'll see where things go between us then. For now, it has to be as it is—you and I are friends, good friends, but nothing more. Please, Ethan, I need you to understand. I need you to just wait until my kid is ready, and I've talked to Frank and Michael, and the clan is more settled. Will you just be patient?"

Ethan's heart sank into his throat, and he fought to keep his face from betraying him. He coughed once and then said, "Of course, Amber. I've been waiting. I can wait some more. Whatever happens, we're friends. That's what's important."

Amber smiled and hugged him, and Ethan desperately wanted nothing more than for the completion alarm to ring on his computer so he could go home, and bury himself in the endless tasks of the homestead.

- 24 -

1600 HOURS - ZERO DAY +10

CAPTAIN TAGGART LOOKED around the living room of the apartment. After meeting Mr. Black at the bridge, they'd fled further south, dodging patrols and hiding from drones. Black had eventually led him to this place, along with Eagan and a handful of Militia members and Black's own men, who were all tattooed Latinos. Before the war, they were scum, thugs and gangsters, but now Taggart found himself fighting alongside them, and his respect for the gangsters had grown after seeing them fight and die for each other. In a way, life for them must have been much like the military life for Taggart; the gang was their family as much as the unit was for Taggart. Maybe more so. And if regulations, or laws, got in the way of protecting their gang, those regs got sidestepped. Most of them would have made good soldiers if they could have just knocked the chips off their shoulders.

"So this is all we have left?" asked Taggart. "Me, Eagan, Black and Chongo, four Militia and six gangbangers?"

"Yes and no," replied Black. "I was able to contact two of my other lieutenants, like Chongo here, and they're in other backup safe houses nearby. Between them, they got six soldiers, eight of my gang, and five Militia guys. We all got guns, and the safe houses have ammo and food just like this one, yo."

"So we have you and me, seventeen of your gang, seven soldiers, and nine Militia. Thirty-five people in total. How many did we lose?"

"I don't know. Most of my crew know the hideouts, and they all got radios in 'em. If any my boys survived, they'll straggle in over the next few hours, hopefully with more of you soldiers and them Militia guys."

Taggart nodded and said, "So, now that we're not running for our lives, who the hell attacked us? They weren't invading soldiers."

Chongo shrugged. "Those were Spyder's crew. He was small time before the 'vaders came. The 20s warned us he had bitched out and gone traitor, working with the enemy, and that he took over all the turf around him. And everyone knows he was using slaves to build his rubble wall around his territory. It was a matter of time before he came after Angel's turf."

Black shot a withering look at Chongo, who looked down immediately.

Eagan didn't notice the slip, apparently, and said, "Yeah, but he had rocket launchers and AKs. So, the enemy must have given him all that hardware and set 'em loose on your 'hood,' Black."

Black—or Angel—nodded. "He's wanted my hood forever, but was too much of a bitch to take it. The invaders must have known something was going on in my hood with the Resistance, so they just encouraged Spyder to come take it. Spyder don't give two shits about the invaders or the Resistance, though—I figure he just wanted to spread his empire. He'll get his, though, just as soon as the 'vaders decide he got too 'big time.' No way that fool gonna take too much bowing and scraping to no ragheads. Sooner or later, they gonna waste his ass."

Taggart filed the name "Angel" away for future reference. Mr. Black was the name he'd heard from his cousin, Dimitri, God rest his soul, before Black, or rather Black's boss, had killed him. But that was in another world, a world with lights and microwaves, a world in which Taggart and Black weren't just about the only thing getting in the way of the conquest of the United States. A better world. Fuck it, back to today. Right now, the Mission mattered more than Taggart's personal bullshit.

"For right now, though," said Taggart, "he did what the invaders couldn't, and disrupted the Resistance in this entire neighborhood. That gives the enemy breathing room to get their conquest back on track, and even send some soldiers from here to back up their forces in other neighborhoods. We need to figure out how to put some pressure back on these assholes so they can't do that."

Chongo's radio crackled: "Boss, yo, we got company."

Taggart caught the panic in the man's voice, and rushed to the window, along with Black, and pulled the edge of the drapes aside enough to peer out, then his jaw dropped. Down in the street below, five quad-copter drones hovered, each at an intersection with various alleyways that opened onto the safe house's street.

Behind him, Taggart heard the men and women in the apartment readying their weapons, but he was more interested in the scene outside. His adrenaline began to rise. Five drones was no coincidence. And then another drone, larger than the five, streaked over the roof of a nearby house —more of a shack by Taggart's way of thinking—and it must have caught sight of Taggart or Black in the window, because it came to a halt and hovered a mere fifty feet from them, directly level with their third-floor apartment.

Then, the strangest thing happened. The other five drones approached and rose up behind the large drone, like the heads of a hydra, and Taggart saw that they had what looked like miniature Gatling guns mounted on their undersides. The guns swiveled toward the drone—and Taggart, on the other side of it—and he saw them spit fire.

Taggart cried, "Get down!" and hit the deck. He heard the staccato noise of tiny machine guns, and then the simultaneous noises of the window shattering and a small explosion. After that, silence. He counted slowly to ten, then risked rising up just enough to peer out from the bottom edge of the window, trying to avoid the shards of glass that had rained down all around him.

For the second time in only moments, Taggart was surprised. The five drones still hovered, but their miniature guns no longer pointed in his direction. The larger drone lay on the street below, smoke rising from its shattered form. Other drones, identical to the first five, began to emerge from other alleyways and street intersections. Taggart stopped counting after a dozen. But why had they destroyed the big drone, and why did they then stand down?

Black cried out, "Look, below! Mi soldatos!"

Taggart glanced at whatever Black was looking at and saw that, from each of the alleys and street corners, men and women were emerging cautiously, armed with M4s and other weapons. Most wore "gangster" clothes, some wore 5.11-style BDU pants and polo shirts, and still others wore Army-issue BDU uniforms. They were gangbangers, Militia members, and soldiers, clearly. And there were a lot of them. The drones had miraculously led these men and women to Black and Taggart.

Taggart grinned. "I don't know who's doing it, but we have an ally somewhere, helping us. They brought together our survivors and rallied them to us. So, Black, now that we have an army again, what's the Resistance going to do?"

Black clenched his jaw and said in a voice so menacing that Taggart shifted to look at him by pure reflex, "Only the 20s could have done this. And we're gonna do what I should have done in the first place. We're gonna kill some motherfuckers who need killin'."

Taggart heard Eagan behind him laugh and shout, "About damn time," and the other men and women in the apartment cheered.

* * *

2000 HOURS - ZERO DAY +10

Ethan, again working with Cassy, had set up the antenna and rig in a new location. As before, one of the Marines stood guard while Ethan prepared his broadcast and settled in to begin. In short order, he had received an updated file from the 20s, labeled "Urgent." It again contained the cryptic phrase about Operation Backdraft being a go, and curiosity ate at him, but he didn't know where to begin looking, much less how to identify and crack any real data. Unanswerable questions drove Ethan nuts. But, time enough to ponder that later. The update also included vital new information for the Resistance groups. For now, despite the risk, he had a job to do.

A few minutes later the radio was transmitting on loop, and there was little to do while they waited the allotted run time. He turned to Cassy. "So what did Michael say about the security of the place? I know you had him and his team getting familiar with the property and taking notes."

"They met with Frank an hour ago. I went to the meeting, but only because I know the property better than anyone. Despite what people seem to think, Frank's our fearless leader. I just run the farm itself because I'm the one best qualified for that job. I set the place up."

Ethan shook his head. "Don't be ridiculous, Cassy. You may say Frank's in charge, but everyone—the new Marines included—understand that this is now your show. Frank is your Foreman."

"Well, I refuse the crown. Frank started this clan thing, and we all know and trust him. He's the best one to lead. And he's smart enough to tap the knowledge of others. Me for farming, Michael for security, and so on."

"Bah. I was there when *you* tapped Michael to lead the security team. But anyway, what did Mike say during the meeting?"

Cassy frowned for a couple seconds, then seemed to shake herself loose of whatever thoughts she was having. Finally, she said, "Well, the house is secure and has good cover. It's made of sandbags, or actually from what we call 'earthbags.' We lay out sandbags with a sand-and-clay mix, like bricks. We offset each layer from the one before, then we cover it with chicken wire and then with adobe."

"Right, I remember you talking about that. Michael says it should stop a .50 caliber round. But the rest of the property?"

"Firstly, there's not enough room and having everyone in one small house is dangerous. He thinks we should spend the winter building more earthbag homes, clustered together around a common area for kids and cooking and whatever, and all of it surrounded with an earthbag wall. Eventually two concentric walls with dirt between them, but that'll be a huge job."

Ethan nodded. More houses made sense and a moderately covered area between them would make a great common area. He filed it away for later thought and waited for Cassy to continue.

"Also, he says the barbwire fence around the property is a good start but won't stop anyone who's serious about coming in. Won't even slow them down much. He noticed that the pathways throughout the property all flow outward from the house, getting more narrow as they branch out to various areas like the veins of a leaf. He'd never seen that before, but from a natural farming point of view, it makes perfect sense. It's efficient and uses minimal land for pathways. But it also means that everything else is like an overgrown temperate-climate jungle. Anyone infiltrating will almost have to follow the pathways."

"Yeah…" said Ethan, his voice fading as his mind raced through possibilities. Cassy's layout had unintentionally given the property built-in choke points, which could be used to funnel any intruders into a smaller number of places. "What's he want to do with them?"

"He wants to find a location that spots the major outlying hubs where paths come together, and build a tower there. It would be where he posts up the guard. He thinks it should be manned 24/7 by someone with a radio, and the guards should check in frequently. But he also thinks we should set up booby traps along the hubs, which are all *behind* the house, to slow attackers and alert us to their presence."

Ethan nodded. "Smart. Homemade mines and alarms are easy to make and set up. We just need to ensure *we all* know where they are. We can mark them in a discreet way, like maybe with small rock piles."

Cassy grinned. "Yeah, I know a lot about improvised mines and such. I did a lot of research. I guess it's a prepper thing, but yeah, I'm prepped. You seem to be, also. We can work on the design together if you want."

Damn straight Ethan wanted to. Two heads were better than one, and he'd sleep better knowing the intimate details of their passive security measures—the things that didn't require a human to operate them. "Awesome, yeah. But did Michael say anything about the neighbors or threats in the area?"

Cassy looked at her feet, lips pursed as her brow furrowed. "Yes. And it's mixed news. The neighbors are either friendly to me or missing. Michael thinks we can move the neighbors into our planned compound and integrate their lands with ours if they want or simply do it if the owners are missing. Grow the community, gain extra skills, and so on. It's a good idea. But the bad news is that he found evidence of what I can only describe as raiders. Burnt homesteads with corpses around like they were ambushed. Traces of at least a dozen attackers, he says, judging by the footprints and other traces. But Ethan, the worst thing—and you can't say anything to the others about this because I swore secrecy—is that the bodies were missing some... Parts were gone. Buttocks, calves, thighs, and ribs, all gone."

Ethan whistled, and the color drained from his face as he thought it out. "They were *butchered?* Are you saying these raiders are freakin' *cannibals?*"

Cassy nodded glumly. "Yeah, that's a possibility, but Michael doesn't think they're cannibals. He says it's 'PsyOps,' meant to terrify the people who are in the area so the raiders don't have to work so hard at their looting. If people are terrified, they flee more than fight, and if they do fight, then they break morale easier. Anyway, Frank's going to announce it all when we know more, but Michael says that for the moment they won't attack a group as large as ours, just so long as we don't make ourselves look like easy pickings."

"Thus the traps, alarms, and guard tower..."

"Yeah. But you should have seen Michael when he told me and Frank. He was iron-jawed angry but looked very sure of himself when he said they wouldn't attack us. They'll pick off our neighbors first, which is what they're already doing, and which is why he wants us to invite the neighbors to join the clan, or at least move in under our protection and help make everybody more secure."

Ethan grinned. "Well, seems we have a plan to deal with the apparent cannibal threat, and in the meantime we have goals. Plans for the future. Something to unify us all and give us a purpose. The kids will grow up knowing what it is to be attuned to the farm, the plants and animals, the extended family, all that. Right? And we're out of the way, not likely to be found by the invaders. Even better, there's a huge forest north of us with plenty of hunting and maybe also raw materials. Turns out you saved us with this farm, Cassy, just as much as the clan ever saved you."

Ethan leaned back on his elbows, enjoying the last bit of sunshine and the moment of quiet. The most recent file from the 20s showed partisan units all over Pennsylvania and New York going on a guerrilla counter-attack, and he had high hopes for whatever this Operation Backdraft was. They'd said they would need his help later to make the Operation successful, but that would be another time. For now, though he suspected it was just a window or the eye of the storm, he was happy to share the clan's peace and plenty.

The world was dying all around them, but here they had found a new home, and he knew they'd all fight to protect that. "It's a dark new world, you once said, Cassy, but maybe it doesn't have to be a bad one."

The future looked bright for now, and his thoughts turned as usual to Amber and the life they might share here. He realized that maybe for the first time since the old ways came down around their ears, he felt like they all just might have a good future ahead. The thought brought a quiet smile.

- 25 -

2100 HOURS - ZERO DAY +10

THE SUN WAS going down as Peter watched increasingly familiar landscape roll by through the passenger window of Jim's car, and his excitement grew. What a stroke of luck it was to find Jim and his car and to earn a ride by saving the man's life. After spending hours in the car talking about a million different things, Peter now had a competent-looking ally. Jim didn't much like women, but who could blame him? The man had tried to help a woman right after the lights went out, and she'd repaid him by plotting to kill him. Jim got her gun away from her when she wasn't looking but had been stabbed in the thigh as a result, and she'd laughed as she left him bleeding out and begging for his life.

Other than that, though, Jim seemed like a great guy, a hard worker who understood loyalty and the need to adapt with the times. Practical, that's what Jim was, and Peter needed men like that by his side. Jim, for his part, seemed to really take a shine to Peter's description of the White Stag Farms community, what they stood for, and how they had rallied together to protect themselves and their families from the shit-storm of chaos that was swirling all around them.

"Something ahead," said Jim, and Peter snapped his attention back to the road. They were approaching a long, slow rise, and at the crest of the hill was some sort of roadblock. Peter saw armed men behind the makeshift barricade.

"Don't worry about it. Those are my people. They must have pulled back all the way to here due to the brown haze. Most of our land is poisoned now, it seems. I wonder how many are still alive after the planes bombed the compounds? Just approach slowly and stop when they say to."

Jim slowed to about ten miles per hour and approached. When they were a hundred feet away someone with a megaphone shouted, "Stop the vehicle, and exit with your hands up." At the same time, a man and a woman with hunting rifles emerged from behind the barricade with their weapons pointed at the windshield.

"You sure about this, mister?" Jim asked.

As he opened the passenger door, Peter said, "Yes. Just get out and keep your hands up. I'll do the talking. We'll be through the checkpoint in no time."

The armed man approached Peter and Jim, and stared. "Well I'll be. Peter, you made it back alive, you old son of a gun. When your scouts came back, they said you were chasing some spy or something. They said you'd be back."

"Good to see you too, Ed. Yeah, I was on a chase, but that's done. How many of us made it through the bombing? Who's leading us?"

"Robert's dead. We're being led by a council of the four remaining Supervisors right now. Only about fifty of us made it through the bombing and the brown haze they sprayed. All the crops are dead and so's our grain mill. We got supplies, but not enough left for winter even with half of us dead."

Peter nodded. It was as bad as he'd feared. "Well, I'm back now, and I got the answer to our problems. I'm going to lead us out of this wasteland and bring us to a place we can rebuild from."

"Oh yeah? Damn, Peter, that's a relief. The council wants to stay, but just about no one else does. People are tense, Peter. Tread lightly, okay?"

Peter shook his head. "I'm done treading lightly. I have the solution to our problem, and people will want to go instead of dying over the corpse of White Stag Farms. If the council won't give in, they can damn well stay here by themselves. Go get everyone together, so's I can talk to them all at once."

"You got it, boss," said Ed with a grin, and rode off.

Peter turned to Jim. "The Supervisors are a rough bunch and used to getting their way. I need you to watch my back, a right-hand man. Want the job?"

Jim paused. "Yeah, Peter. Let's do it. I have your back."

Peter smiled and waited for word the people were assembled. This was his time, Peter's time to shine. And God help anyone who got in the way of him saving these people.

An hour later, as they drove into the remains of the White Stag compound, he saw his people's survivors waiting for him. The Supervisors stood separately with their own supporters, only ten in all. Most of the rest—the smarter ones, forty or so—stood waiting for his arrival.

Peter felt his heart beating faster, almost giddy in fact. Show time. He stepped out of the car and raised his arms, grinning. "My people," he roared, voice soaring over the crowd, and they settled into whispers. "You know that when I left this place with my scouts, it was before the bombing. We were chasing the spy who had killed one of us, but she evaded us. She called in the enemy and was responsible for the deaths of Robert and half our people of the Farms. But I would not let her get away, no. I tracked her to her lair, she and all her people."

He paused, scowling to let his anger show, then continued. "They led the enemy to us so their own lands would be safe, but she made a mistake, because so long as any of us live she can never sleep soundly. I'm coming for her, and I'll take payment for our land and lives by taking hers for ourselves. We were her victims"—he raised his fists dramatically—"but we survived!"

Again he paused, hearing some of the people yelling "Yes!" and "You're right!" and "Our turn!"

Satisfied that he had them with him, he dropped his arms and continued in a more informational voice, pleased at how they all quieted down as soon as he spoke again. "Her land is rich," he said, "full of crops and fruit trees. She commands the farms around her too, with more cattle than I could count and hundreds of ripe acres. Houses that weren't bombed. Silos that never got burned to the ground. There's enough to take our families not just through the winter but all the way to next harvest. The neighbors support her, so I'm coming for them, too."

Again he raised his voice. "And I'm bringing my people with me!"

When Peter mentioned the spy and the death of their people, the crowd had grown angry, but their faces began to light up with hope as he described the rich lands awaiting them.

When he stopped speaking, his people cheered—all but the Supervisors and their followers. They were looking angry.

One Supervisor, a gray-haired man in his fifties with sharp, angular features under a leather cowboy hat, spat and took a step toward Peter. "Who the hell are you to say what we're gonna do," he bellowed, looking determined. "You're not in charge here, Peter. This is our land, these are our supplies. Not one kernel of corn goes with anyone who leaves." He glared at Peter. "We took you in ten years ago,

Peter. We gave you a place to stay, fed you, helped you get back on your feet. You repay us by trying to take everyone *out there?* They'll die out there. Here, they have food. This season's a bust, but next year we'll grow more. This is our home, Peter. Most of us were born in these parts, and now you want them to leave?"

And then he made his declaration: "I'll die before I let you lead them out into that storm, Peter. You're under arrest."

The Supervisor motioned with his head, and two men with rifles left the Supervisors' group and walked toward Peter. The rest of the crowd looked on, many showing defeat in their eyes already. This was not how Peter had planned it. Damn it, this was not his destiny.

Peter formed a pistol shape with his index finger and thumb, pointed it at the supervisor, and lowered his thumb as though firing. Then, a shot rang out. The Supervisor looked stunned and confused as a crimson blossom appeared on his chest and rapidly spread. Then he fell like a tree and moved no more. Another shot rang out, and one gunman's head snapped back, brains and gore splattering the ground behind him as he fell. The other gunman dropped his rifle and showed his empty hands.

Peter shook his head sorrowfully at the gray-haired corpse. "Sorry, boss," he said, "but you called it. I won't let you murder my people by forcing them to stay." He turned to the rest of the Supervisors group, who were looking around frantically for the source of the shots, but Peter wasn't worried. He'd made sure Jim was well hidden before he had even pulled up to the dying farm's gate. It was a precaution Peter had approved "just in case," and now he was damned glad he and Jim had thought of it.

Peter raised his gaze to the forty who still waited for him to speak. They looked a bit more nervous now. "The rest of you have two choices. You can stay here and let my people take only what we need to get to the farms—and we will take it—or you can follow me to the richer land. My people will take only what we need to get there, and we'll leave the rest for those who choose to stay." He turned to the Supervisor group. "Either way, you Supervisors aren't in charge anymore, and you aren't going to let those who leave die of starvation for making that choice. If you can't bear to give up what ain't yours, draw down on me, and we'll end your worries for you." He took on a reasonable tone and showed them empty palms, the ancient signal of peaceful intent. "Look, the boss paid you to be in charge before the lights went out but this isn't that world anymore. The boss who paid you is dead. No one's paying anybody anymore. So, you decide. Stay and lead a dying farm, or come with us to something better."

One by one, the henchmen of the Supervisors walked over to join the larger group. Finally, only three Supervisors remained. One said, "Aw hell, Peter. I guess we just elected you Foreman. I hope these farms you talk about are everything you say, but they have to be better than here. I'm in."

The other two nodded, and Peter smiled at them, friendly and welcoming. "Good. Our people can use your hands, and we need your experience. For our people, I welcome you back among us."

Then he turned to the crowd and grinned his triumph. "Let's get to bed, people. In the morning, we got work to do. It's a long way to go, but we're gonna take what we deserve when we get there. Those people cost us our land, our families, and our friends, so they're gonna make it right by giving us theirs. And don't worry. I won't let my people starve."

Peter saw real hope on their faces for the first time since

he'd returned, and swore he wouldn't let them down. Nothing and no one would stand in his way.

# # #

* * * * * * * * * * * * * * * * * *

For a **SNEAK PEEK** of Book Three
in the Dark New World series,
please visit: **bit.ly/dnw3sneakpeek**

* * * * * * * * * * * * * * * * * *

About the authors:

JJ Holden lives in a small cabin in the middle of nowhere. He spends his days studying the past, enjoying the present, and pondering the future.

Henry Gene Foster resides far away from the general population, waiting for the day his prepper skills will prove invaluable. In the meantime, he focuses on helping others discover that history does indeed repeat itself and that it's never too soon to prepare for the worst.

For updates, new release notifications, and more, please visit:

www.jjholdenbooks.com

Printed in Great Britain
by Amazon